The Tackle Box:
Stories About People
Who Fish

Large Print Edition

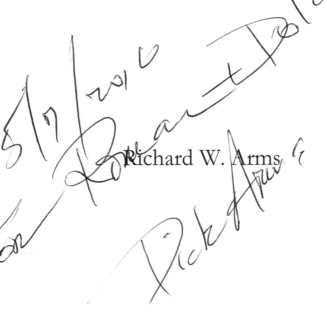

Richard W. Arms

ISBN: 0692696571
ISBN-13: 978-0692696576

BELFORT & BASTION

Publishers For This Millennium

BelfortandBastion.com

Cover photo: James DeMers
pixabay.com/en/tackle-box-fishing-supplies-695271/
Cover design: Michael Jay Tucker

CONTENTS

To Mercedes,
who listened to each story and provided both
support and advice.

INTRODUCTION

Among the most essential items for any fisherman is his tackle box. Be he fishing for Bluegills of Bluefin Tuna, brook trout, lake Trout or Sea Trout, the tackle box is always nearby, in the bottom of the boat or up on the grassy bank. The fisherman opens the cover, reaches down and selects a lure. It gives him pleasure to pick out a favorite, one that he has used often before. He likes it because he thinks the fish like it. This collection of stories is intended to be like a tackle box. Reach down and pick one out, perhaps trying out a new one or perhaps going back to one that gave pleasure before. As with the fishing tackle, the stories are meant for many different conditions and many different kinds of fishermen. Perhaps a trout fisherman will prefer "Old Ike" while a Salt Water fisherman will prefer "Turn of the Tide", but I anticipate that fishermen are fishermen, and will want to delve into many aspects.

Please, though, do not think that this book will teach you anything about fishing. That is not the intent. It is not a collection of tales about fishing, it is a collection of tales about people who fish. Men, women children. Be they on a trout stream or a yacht, they have the common trait that they enjoy fishing. These are stories about some of those people.

I believe that people who fish are not very different from normal human beings. They may have an obsession, but so does the stamp collector or the baseball fan. But fishing does bring out character in the participants. When you are standing in a boat, casting for Smallmouth Bass the fish, sculling his fins at the edge of a patch of weeds, watching for some food to attack, has no idea if you are a woman in a bikini, a boy in jeans or an elderly gentleman wearing a suit from Brooks Brothers, and he doesn't care. If the lure is put in the right place, has the right action and is correctly matched to what he has been eating he may fall for the ruse. The more expensive equipment may help the angler, but it certainly does not promise success. That is why, in one story, I call fishing the great leveler. Fishing is not as interesting, I believe, as the people who do the fishing. To learn about where and when to fish and what tackle and bait to use, there are many magazines and books that can provide that. I am writing about the people who I have observed in a lifetime of fishing, anywhere any time, whenever the opportunity arose. It is the joys and pains of humanity that I like to write about. Fishing has provided many opportunities to observe those people.

Moreover, I have observed that Fishing seems to bring out the best in most people. Perhaps it is because pretense has no rewards. In the story "Catcher on the Ice" we see that there can be a comradery even within the competition. When I see the delight in the smile of a father when his small daughter lands a fish, or the disappointment in a mother who watches a son lose one, I realize that there has been a mutual experience drawing them together. When you get to the end of the story "Old Buddies" you will see the same feelings among grown men. Rarely do we actually encounter the competitive dislike shown by the characters in "Unhooked", and we realize that it was not the fishing that was the cause. In the story "The Brass Bed" we have a contrast between the fisherman and the non-fisherman. In the tale called "The Ministry" we even see the therapeutic value of fishing, although here perhaps other factors play a major role.

In this group of stories I have attempted to cover a broad spectrum of people, and used fishing as the backdrop more than the foreground. I have gone from the early exciting first fishing experience of a young person all the way to sad days when an angler gets too old to fish. Within that I have tried to trace the emotions of those people at the various stages of their lives. To do this I have used many personal experiences, but also included purely fictional stories. "Abuelito" is the most autobiographical of the entries and is therefore near the beginning. The old man in

"The last Marlin" is also me, but observed by another. Sometimes I tell a story and at other times a disinterested observer tells what was happening.

Please lift he lid of "The Tackle Box", look at the assortment of lures I have put in the various trays, select one that appears appetizing and tie it on your line.

DICK ARMS
September 2015

THE TACKLE BOX

I didn't even know where it came from at first. I was finally getting around to cleaning out some shelves in the far corner of the garage. I had put it off for years, but I needed the space, and the old boxes of financial records needed to be shredded in order to make room for newer versions of the same sort of things; those things that you feel you need to keep but that you will actually never look at again. So on rare occasions you get rid of the oldest and least important. That was what I was finally doing when I came across the old tackle box. It was back behind the boxes, hidden from view these many years. I looked at it in wonderment and puzzlement. It had a familiar appearance but I knew it had never been mine. Fishermen know their equipment intimately, and make choices that reflect their preferences. I had never used that tackle box and I never would have bought it. It was too big, too heavy, too old-fashioned. Yet there was something familiar about it.

Pleasantly using it as a diversion from my chore I took it off the shelf and carried it across to my workbench. It was a made of steel, once painted dark green but now largely just a rusty brown that left dusty smears on my jeans.. A clasp at the top, under the handle that had probably once been covered with leather but was now just metal, held the two sections of the domed top together. I could see that if I could lift the front of the clasp and undo the fastener the two sections of the top would swing out, revealing the interior of the tackle box. But the thick rust had solidified it to a mass of reddish brown. Finally with screwdriver, wire brush and pliers, I was able to pry it open and then wedge the two halves of the lid apart. Suddenly, out of the box burst a flood of odors, and with them a wave of memories, and I knew immediately what it was.

What first assailed me was not what I saw but what I smelled. It was the smell of "bug juice"; citronella. And also, more subtle, the smell of pipe tobacco. It was the dusty smell bridging a gap of many years before, yet it brought back a deluge of memories. It was the smell of fishing camps in the woods, and the smell of wood smoke from a fireplace. I may not have really smelled it but I thought I detected Scotch whisky, and burned hotdogs and maybe even grilled steaks. It was the aroma of wet woolen sweaters and rubber boots drying in a corner. Here I had again found Harry. It was not the Harry of the Country Club or the Harry of the Cadillacs, which were all he would condescend to drive. It was the other Harry. It was the Harry when he became what I imagined he wished he was.

I didn't need to even open the box further to know what I would find, but I did manage to pry the lids up. It was as I anticipated. There were three salmon fly fishing reels, manual of course. Harry would never have used an automatic reel. There were boxes of streamer flies and a number of prepared leaders. I saw extra fly lines, line dressing, reel oil in a metal tube and a hook sharpener. Looking further I encountered the inevitable pouch of pipe tobacco, and even a package of pipe cleaners. A pair of pliers too rusted to open and a pocketknife in similar condition. There was little order to the arrangement of the contents. Here Harry was able to allow disorder, because this was the other Harry.

This tackle box was from another era, a time before I had married Harry's daughter. In later years I fished with Harry, but I knew it was not the same as his Maine fishing trips with "the boys" as he referred to them. Yet I thought I got to know Harry so well in the next forty years that I could feel what that box had meant to him We fished in Mexico and we fished in Colorado, We fished the tidewaters in Maine and the coves on Cape Cod. We fished for trout in New Mexico and Mackerel in the Damariscotta River and yellowtail in the Gulf of California. But the Salmon fishing at Rangeley Lake was before my time and it was something special that he only obliquely referenced from time to time. Yet here, in this tackle box, I sensed that I had opened again a very special part of Harry's life, and that I could at least in a small part recall what I had come to understand of Harry because of it.

There is something about fishing that brings out the underlying genuineness of a person, I believe. Perhaps it is a primitive and instinctive thing, wherein the hunter or the fisherman in early times when occupied in these tasks was only concerned with his own preservation and needy of self-reliance. I know that no amount of money, influence, position of importance, worldly accomplishments, or even piety can influence whether that fish is going to gobble a worm or rise to a fly. A trout does not care whether you are wearing blue jeans or a tuxedo. The Striped Bass or Bluefish does not care if you are in a canoe or a yacht. Beautiful people don't catch more fish than ugly ones. The indifference of the quarry makes us abandon our posturing and pretexts. Or so it seemed with Harry.

Harry was a success. Harry was moderately wealthy. Not rich, but well off enough to do what he wanted to in his spare time. And what Harry wanted to do in his spare time was go fishing. Not catch fish, although that added to the pleasure., but just go fishing. And, moreover, although he would condescend in later years to fish any small lake or large bay, his real love was to go fishing in such a way that it became a ritual. To Harry, who had a disdain for organized religion, perhaps because of a religious upbringing, fishing brought back that participation in a liturgy. He who had once been an alter boy now served at the alter of Isaac Walton. And that ritualistic fishing entailed going with a group of men who also worshiped at the same altar. There were very well delineated parameters in a men's fishing camp. They entailed not only actually fishing, but included plaid woolen shirts, chest waders, grilled steaks, moderate drinking, pipe smoking and, most of all the green tackle box. The fishing rod had to be split bamboo in those days, and preferably made in England or Scotland of Tonkin cane. You tied your own flies in the winter, and had a couple of boxes of them ready to go. Only fishing bought out these factors that I came to believe were the real Harry. And the smells and sights from that tackle box encompassed what I thought of as the real Harry, that I had come to know and respect.

I too in later years had participated in similar rituals. In Alaska, fishing for halibut and Salmon off Prince of Wales Island I had experienced the same bonding of fishermen. All the others at the lodge were from very prosaic lives, as was I, I am sure. But there was no discussion of families, or jobs of educations or careers of aspirations. We were fishermen, joined together in the primitive ritual of seeking to outwit fish. That other life was out of bounds. We discussed the waters and the baits and the weather, and the outlook for the next day. We spoke of the talent of lack of talent of the skippers of the boats we were fishing from. We boasted of big ones caught and bemoaned even bigger ones lost.

Such I envisioned, had to have been the atmosphere at that remote fishing camp in Maine, many years before I had even met Harry. "The Boys" were, like Harry, businessmen. But they were there to fish. I wondered if maybe Harry clung to this group with its illusion of remoteness and independence. The masculine bonding would have appealed to him. Harry's success in that other world he was escaping from, although undoubtedly well earned, had come from taking over and becoming president of a company his father had founded. I wondered if he might have felt a little apologetic that his success might be questioned for that reason. Certainly the ground rules of the fishing camp allowed him to put those feeling aside. I am sure he did not mention his family and his wealth just as the others did not.. Yes, this tackle box told a very interesting story about a man I had come to think I had understood. So now, years later, I was standing at my workbench in my garage., smelling and feeling the contents of his tackle box, and remembering my father in law, now gone a number of years. I was sure that I understood this man. He had gone off on his fishing trips with "The Boys" and become., I believed, the underlying person who he really was, separated from, the cares he left behind.

Thinking these thoughts, I was looking down into the scattered debris in the box. I noticed a small metal can that had once held some sort of lozenges, perhaps cough drops, since Harry was always prepared for any medical emergency. It was at the bottom of the box, covered by, and seemingly hidden by, two boxes of flies. I lifted it out of the tackle box and shaking it heard something rustling inside. No doubt a lure or some flies I thought, but the lid was rusted closed. No amount of twisting or banging would let me pry off the cover. Were these, I wondered, his special flies; his secret weapons? Did he hide them at the bottom of the tackle box, to keep them from the curious eyes of his companions; "The Boys"? It seemed a secret I wanted to understand.

There is little that can withstand the combination of WD-40 and a large pair of vise grips. It took a while but I finally was able to twist the metal cover and break it loose from its coating of rust. Lifting it up and peering into the can there was little to see except a dim grey rectangle of heavy paper. I reached in and carefully brought it out. Under it was a small lock of hair, tied with a faded pale blue ribbon. Lifting the paper to the light I realized it was a small faded photograph. It was of a young girl, perhaps ten years old, with brown hair that seemed to match the color of the wisp with the ribbon. I suddenly realized that this was a picture of the little girl who would one day become my wife.

ABUELITO

That's what my kids used to call him, Abuelito, which means, in Spanish, little old Grandfather. It was a name he received on a trip, over a half a century ago, to Mexico. We had been searching for a distinctive name that my new daughter, our first child, could use for my father. The waiter in the cantina on the beach, where we had stopped around noon for a sandwich and a beer, had suggested quietly to me that my wife and I might like to come back that evening for music, dancing and socializing with the locals. But he had looked at my greying father and said, "Pero no traiga Abuelito" meaning, " But don't bring the old man." Aha! Perfect, I thought. It even tied in with the fact that our entire family spoke fluent Spanish, not because of heritage but because we have spent so many years living in Latin America. The name stuck. He became Abuelito to the entire family.

The children as they grew up, were ecstatic when they were taken to visit their Cape Cod grandparents. "Grammy Cape" also doted on them but the routines with Abuelito captivated them. The first thing required in the morning was to set up the coffee pot and start it going, Then they had to go to the Post Office and store to get the morning paper and pick up the mail. On return, a cup of coffee for Abuelito and hot chocolate for the kids. Next they had to raise the flag, and that was followed by feeding the birds. A while later they could take a cup of coffee, with cream and sugar, to Grammy Cape. After that there was always a plan for the day. No time was to be wasted. Perhaps they would take the skiff and outboard way up the harbor and weave among the exposed islands of eelgrass and mud, if the tide was to be low around midday, and dig for clams or quahogs. If the tide was high they might go out to the outer beach for swimming, and with Abuelito's avid participation, try to build up sand barriers to stop the coming tide. Maybe they would go out on the sand dunes and all roll down them, something no longer allowed by law, or perhaps they would, again depending upon the tide, motor way up harbor to the hidden wharf between the sand bars and go blueberrying. There had to be drives to take the trash to the dump, where the seagulls were so numerous they looked like litter themselves, or perhaps a trip to the feed store to get more birdseed. This was the Abuelito my children knew.

The father I knew, the father of prior years, was a sterner and more demanding parent. Yet he was a man who I not only respected and admired, but loved, although I probably never really told him so. With my children he played, almost like a child himself. He took them to buy kites and then we would all fly them from the front yard of his home on a hill, with the breeze always off the bay. When I was a boy he had been an instructor a guide and a mentor, but not a playmate. Rather than just fly a store-bought kite, in

Cuba when I was only five years old I remember him helping to make a kite out of bamboo strips, newspaper, paste made with flour and water, and a tail made of old rags. Then he taught us, my older brother Charlie and me, how one of us could hold the kite while the other took the string and ran with it to launch it into the sky. At that time I was still the kite holder, but in later years I would be allowed to do the running. I can picture him still, as he was in those days. He was tall, and quite thin. Even then his New England face had become very red from constant exposure to the tropic sun. He wore, nearly always, khaki trousers and a matching open collared shirt, and a wide brimmed hat. He had a mare he used to ride out into the sugarcane fields to inspect the crops and supervise the supervisors. It seemed like the tallest horse I had ever seen, and with my dad up on top of it looking down Dad was a giant; but a giant with a smile.

It was in Cuba that Dad first taught me how to fish, if you could consider it fishing. As the administrator of the sugar mill, a small one consisting of the mill surrounded by huge fields of growing sugarcane, the offices, the homes for the workers and a small *tienda*, all located in nearly the exact geographic center of Cuba, he was provided with a large white very colonial looking house of two stories, with verandas all the way around the upper story.   It was in the midst of a grove of Royal palms and a grassy area that might have passed for a lawn. But what was exciting was that there were a number of tarantula holes in that lawn. It was there that Dad helped me to fish for tarantulas. The idea was to tie a small piece of soap on the end of a string and lower it down the hole. After a while you would suddenly yank it upward, and if the tarantula had been wrapped around the soap, eating it, you yanked him out of his hole. I don't think you could feel a bite, as you do with a fish when it takes a bait, but I do remember that we occasionally extracted tarantulas.   We called it fishing, and it was fun. It probably was this entertainment that led to a lifetime of fishing, sometimes with my father and sometimes without.

From ages five to seven we lived in Colombia. It was a sugar mill, again, but this time way up the Magdalena River in a hot humid jungle that came right up to the high walls that surrounded out house. I remember particularly the riverboat that took us there. It was a white, narrow beamed and high bowed boat that only lacked Humphrey Bogart and Katherine Hepburn to have passed for the African Queen. My mother was covered in light clothes to protect her from the sun and sat in a deck chair, fanning herself to not only keep cool but to drive off the numerous flies, mosquitoes and other flying insects. Charlie and I were, of course, all over the boat, looking down at the river, and watching for alligators and imagining piranhas. But I particularly remember Dad, standing by the helmsman, watching the river ahead and looking very nautical. He loved boats and fishing, and may have been picturing being able to stop and cast for Peacock Bass. Even in mid-river there was no breeze and the humidity and heat were oppressive. We were to soon learn that it was a permanent condition there, day or night, and even the tropical showers did little to cool things down. To get to the sugar mill from the river, I vaguely remember a crossing a river in a dugout canoe with paddlers, and then a ride in a motorized track car on railroad tracks that led to the small settlement that served the mill and fields of cane. This was my father's new assignment. Our house was not unlike the one in Cuba, except that it was infested with bats. We had a pet monkey, and could not leave the premises alone because of snakes. Even so, sometimes they got past the ten-foot wall that surrounded the back yard. Our gardener once killed a Bushmaster in the rafters of the unwalled shed that was used by the maid for doing laundry in outside tubs. Our monkey, Pedro, was tied to one of the posts and was panicking and pulling on his chain. The gardener knew what was going on, warned Charlie and me away and knocked it down with a long pole. But Charlie and I were reading Kipling about then and it was all an adventure from those books. We slept in hammocks on the veranda to keep cool and were, of course, taught school by our mother.

It was near the end of the second year there that I acquired one of the most vivid memories of those years. My father had a short wave radio beside his chair, and was in the habit of listening to the news from the States in the early evening. It was a Sunday in December and as usual he had his ear to the radio, trying, through the static, to get the news. Suddenly he jumped up and yelled to my mother to come quickly. It meant nothing to Charlie and me at the time, but he announced loudly that the Japanese had bombed Pearl Harbor.

We returned to the States very soon thereafter. With the world again at war Dad was now too old to go. It was only after his death that we, his children, learned, oddly enough from a veteran's group who wanted to place a plaque on his grave, that he had been an Army private in the First World War. He never wanted to tell us about it, evidently. I realized then how little I really knew about this man, who seemed so open and reachable in the present but was unwilling to speak much about his past. All I really ever knew was that he had finished just two years of agricultural college and then, after a gap in our information, somehow ended up in a very minor job in a sugar mill in Cuba, only to, within three years, become the manager of the same sugar mill. The military service filled a gap. It says a lot that he went, without any degrees, from Army Private to eventually become one of the top people in his profession. But that was not the Dad we knew. Our dad was the man that preceded us to Paraguay for his next job. Now, instead of running a single sugar mill he was upgrading and modernizing and expanding the sugar industry, be it miniscule at the time, of an entire country. He went before us, found us a house, a cook a maid and a gardener, and started to work. It being wartime, though, and transportation in those years far slower and more difficult, it was a trip of nearly two weeks for Charlie, our mother and me, to get there. High-ranking military travelers had priority, so we had to, on one occasion, wait a number of days, after being "bumped" by a ranking officer, for another flight.

Yet much of the trip was the most modern of its day. Train to Florida, then PanAm clipper to Manaus, a key rubber-exporting center, essential to the war effort, in the center of the Amazon rainforest of Brazil.

The Clippers, now looked back on nostalgically in the history of aviation, were four-engine amphibious planes; flying boats whose bodies, when not in the air, rested directly on the water and were balanced by pontoons extending down from the wings. When they took off or landed the water splashed up over the round windows; windows that when we cruised over the Caribbean, were covered by circles of cardboard to stop us from seeing possible convoys below, and perhaps reporting them to the packs of German U-boats that hunted very close to the American mainland. From the top of South America we flew directly over those endless rainforests to Manaus, a seemingly unlikely route for a plane that needs to land on water, but we landed from time to time, on remote rivers with barges at anchor, supplying us with gasoline from barrels.

By comparison, the rest of the trip, DC3's down the Amazon, around the hump of Northeastern Brazil to Rio, and finally to Asuncion, Paraguay was routine for blasé seasoned travelers as Charlie and I considered ourselves. We had flown thousands of miles,

Charlie had been taken fishing on the Amazon River, we had slept in hammocks under mosquito netting, we had been walking in zigzags following the curves of the mosaic sidewalks of Copacabana while most of our friends in Massachusetts had never been further than Boston. We did not realize that the world had suddenly changed and that millions of Americans, military and civilians, were now, and would be thereafter, traveling to every part of the world. But for us we were just on our way to another distant place, and this one would be far less remote than the Columbian lowlands.

The entire project in Paraguay was a philanthropic effort, designed to help a backward country improve its economy. There were American consultants in many different fields, from manufacturing to dairy farming. Dad was the expert on sugarcane and sugar production, which entailed consulting and helping to implement modernization of the industry. Moreover there were hopes of expanding the production to the northern hinterlands, the region approaching the Matto Grosso. Charlie and

I went to a real school in Asuncion, although it was all conducted in Spanish. It was a tough school and did not cater to the few Americans that attended. When my friend Petey and I played hooky and were found out the Headmaster spanked us both with a wooden paddle, and my father backed him up on the action, hurting both pride and backside a second time. After that we found non-school times to sneak off and smoke horrible looking and terribly strong twisted pieces of tobacco that passed there for cigars. We got so we could smoke two apiece in an afternoon, in the forested area along the Paraguay River, without any sign of turning green, as would have been expected if the usual stories were to be believed. Nobody ever caught us at that, and it was only many years later that Dad and I laughed over my telling about it.

Paraguay had been a home for many Germans before the war, and in those war years nobody knew who might be a Nazi sympathizer. The problem was that many of the very best stores, especially a magnificent hardware store, I recall, were owned by

Germans, some suspected by the embassy of lending financial support to the Axis. Therefore they circulated a blacklist of stores we were asked to not patronize. It was almost a joke within the American community, yet my father was scrupulous in never resorting to those stores, tempting as it might be. Interestingly, before long his closest friends seemed to stop the joking and started to boycott the blacklisted stores also, yet Dad never had made a comment about it. Dad had a way of getting his ideas across without ever having to emphasize them. It worked with his friends, his family and those who worked for him. In later years, looking back, I saw how both my parents were able to instill values without lecturing us. A look of admonition worked just as well in our family as a loud reprimand might have in other families. But we knew that behind the quietness lurked consequences. My mother, if necessary, could apply the back of a hairbrush to a recalcitrant child's rear that, in today's world, might not be acceptable, and reported to the authorities as child abuse, but it certainly worked.

After two years Dad was asked by the same sponsors to tackle a bigger job in Venezuela. In Paraguay the dislike of American, especially reflected in the attitudes of street gangs of native children had led to many confrontations and exciting slingshot battles. Gringo was not a joking term then as it often is now is in America. In Venezuela the conflict was even more intense and difficult. But with conflict comes opportunity to the Arms Dealers. Charlie and I made our spending money selling slingshots we made from old inner tubes and forked sticks, to many of our friends. Certainly our parents must have been aware of the ongoing conflict, but I do not ever remember any commentary on it. Often we would be late to school because of being ambushed on the way and having to wage a running and circuitous battle to get there, but the excuse on late arrival was considered legitimate and acceptable. Our parents were more concerned though when one of the frequent revolutions was in progress. We loved it because school was cancelled during the revolt, but we were confined to our yard, and could only stand by the end of the property and watch the trucks, loaded with rioters' loot go by.

At the end of the war Dad's job ended also, and we were to go home to Massachusetts. But everyone else, it seemed, had the same intentions, and it was impossible to get airline reservations. However, Dad checked around and found that a very small freighter of Dutch registry, was leaving for New York from La Guaira, the port for Caracas, in a few days and that it also carried passengers, but only sixteen. He was able to get us four of those spots.

It was on that exciting, eventful and enlightening freighter trip, a week at sea, that a different and even better father came to light. He seemed to shed all his concerns and just enjoy himself. He participated in whatever we boys wanted to do. Dad was extremely relaxed that first evening out on the ocean, as the ship's captain gave him a fine Dutch cigar, which Dad reveled in smoking as he watched the wake of the ship behind and below our high stateroom. As though joking, I asked Dad for a puff or two on his cigar. Thinking, of course, that it would make me sick and cure me of wanting to smoke, being new to smoking and also at sea, he laughingly handed it to me. After my years of surreptitiously smoking those black stogies with Petey is was the mildest cigar I had ever tried, and was really enjoying it until Dad took it back.

The trip was eventful right from the start. Just after we had cleared port Charlie and I received an introduction to real drama when one of the crew members who had come aboard drunk after shore leave, became belligerent, toward another crew member. As we stood above the deck-well, looking down from on high, we saw him run to the galley, return with a knife and attempt to stab the other man. The second officer, stepping in and trying to stop the fight, was stabbed in the shoulder as we watched, and then we saw the assailant subdued and taken away to confinement of some sort. Attempted murder was certainly exciting. Two days later the culprit was dropped off for trial at the nearest Dutch port, Curacao. Dad looked on it all as a learning experience for me and Charlie, now ages eleven and fourteen., respectively. He was suddenly enjoying the trip and the rest too much to be overly concerned. It was not really a transformation. The same father had always been there, with his sense of humor, his love of people and of life, his concern for his boys, but now he was without cares, it seemed. He delighted in the sea and we had the complete run of the ship, small as it was, and wherever his boys were, Dad was with us, relaxed, smiling, and at times playing with us as we explored every corner. It was while we were still in the southern Caribbean that we discovered a heavy line trailing over the stern of the ship, attached to the railing. Of course we wanted to know what it was, and asked him, believing that he was an expert on all things nautical. With a straight face he told us that they were fishing. Knowing, though, that Dad would never really lie to us but would sometimes kid with us, we were skeptical. At just that time one of the ship's officers, an older Dutch man came by, so dad called him over and told him that he had told us the line was for fishing, and that we would not believe him. Unbeknownst to us at the time, Dad was vigorously winking at the officer, over our heads. So the officer confirmed the fishing story, and told us they often caught large sharks and other fish, some of which could be used by the galley for food. So, we were convinced.

That evening Dad's conscience started to bother him. Even in a joke, he hated dishonesty and felt he had carried it too far. He sat, I remember, in a deck chair outside our staterooms, and told us he had been kidding us. The line, he said, was evidently the ship's log; an instrument trailed behind the ship to measure its speed and distance traveled. They were not really fishing from the back of the ship. He didn't want us to be misled permanently, but he had had his joke. He also told us about winking at the officer who had backed up his story. We all laughed.

Two days later the ship entered the Gulf Stream with its large amount of floating weed. As the small ship laboriously plowed through the ocean we were again exploring the ship and found ourselves at the stern, where the line had been tied to the rail. Because of the seaweed the line had evidently been hauled in by one of the seamen. To our amazement and Dad's chagrin, attached to the end of the line was not a nautical instrument but a large and still baited fishhook.

Dad had a dream. He would return to small town New England and become a businessman, leaving sugar factories and world travel behind. The family home was there, occupied by his mother, my long-widowed grandmother It was a large and very old two story white clapboard house with a slate roof and chimneys at both ends. Frozen foods were, Dad believed, the new post-war trend, and he would be there to cash in on it. Obviously, with most households then still using ice boxes and getting ice delivered twice a week, maybe they would eventually become affluent enough to replace them with refrigerators but people would need to rent frozen food lockers and store their food there. He would provide that service. There would be no way, it was thought, that people would be able to actually afford to have freezers in their own homes. So after a mortgage on the house and a depleted nest egg the locker plant was built and, with an old friend as a partner, in business. Dad learned to be a merchant, a salesman, a butcher and even made his own brand of ice cream.

You need to like people if you want to succeed as a retailer, and Dad certainly liked people. You need to love small town living to thrive in that environment and my parents also loved that. But you need to tolerate a great deal of snow and cold in New England, and they were used to the tropics. Most of all, as a business owner there is no regular paycheck, and they were used to a regular and substantial paycheck. Yet they both delighted in the closeness of large families on both sides, with boisterous Christmas and Thanksgiving gatherings. We boys had grandparents, uncles, aunts and cousins in abundance. After being exotic travelers we settled into being American kids in post war America. I'm sure it was not easy from Dad to go from having hundreds of workers answering to him to having to answer to hundreds of customers who were, at least theoretically, always right. But he did it for the next five years. He did it while Charlie and I were in extremely formative times. He did it with pleasure, because he was living the dream he had envisioned. But I am sure there were times when the dream lost its charm.

The high point of each of those years was, not only for him but for me and Charlie, those two weeks in the middle of August during which we had standing reservations at my aunt's cottage on a difficult to reach point of land on Cape Cod, called Sandy Neck. Our mother did not go, because there was neither electricity nor running water. She wanted to be able to take bathes and read in the evening. Outhouses, itchy skin from salt water bathing, sand on sunburns and damp bedding in cramped quarters did not appeal to her, but we boys, of course, delighted in the conditions. To Dad it was a huge treat; an escape from his business duties. I can picture him and Uncle George, at the end of the day, sitting side by side in the boathouse. There was a Dutch door, with the top open and the bottom closed, looking across the mile of water to the town, and allowing one to watch the boats come and go. To Dad's right was the old icebox, containing soft drinks and beer, and hidden in the back, Dad's bottle of

Scotch. The old wooden icebox, lined with galvanized steel never received a block of ice, but it kept the drinks lukewarm instead of hot, and that was enough. Uncle George sat to his left, and we kids, including one or more cousins could, if we remained quiet, sit in the background. At the end of the day the long shadow of the building would move out over the water or, if the tide was out, over the rocky and shell-strewn sand that was loosely thought of as a beach. The terns and gulls would be picking at crabs between us and the remaining low water in a harbor. If it was high tide it was a huge expanse of water, and at low tide just a channel between immense sand bars. The boathouse was also where I always insisted on sleeping, instead in of in the house, because at high tide, in the middle of the night, you could hear the water sloshing back and forth under the floorboards.

The first year that we went Dad presented us each with a fishing pole. I do not call it a rod, since it was just a single long piece of bamboo, varnished and wrapped with heavy twine for handholds and to secure the guides and reel. It had a rubber cap on the butt that was actually meant to go on a walking cane. It was fitted with a Penn reel without a level wind so I had to learn to guide the green braided line with my thumb while reeling, and of course, it had a star drag. Compared to the expensive rods now in my closet it was primitive, but it was my first salt water rig and I still can remember it. And I certainly put it to work, though with not much success at first. Every few days we had to go to Town for groceries. That meant taking the skiff with its five horsepower outboard, and loading it with about five people and crossing the mile of water to the town landing. The strong tidal currents made it necessary to time it so we went to town on the coming tide and after shopping returned on the going tide, with the boat with even less freeboard because of the weight of the groceries. But that did not stop me from taking my new and precious fishing equipment with me and trolling all the way over and back. But the best I ever did was to hook the anchor chain of the black can buoy that marked the channel as we swept by, propelled by the strong tide flow. I was sure it was a monstrous Striped

Bass. Of course, I was fishing at the wrong place, at the wrong tide at the wrong speed. But Dad let me hope.

But then, the next day, Dad took just me out in the boat, and taught me how to read the water and the birds, and I caught my first Striper. It was perhaps four pounds, but to me it was a giant. Charlie was not with us as he was far more interested in the fact that there was a girls' summer camp just down the beach from Aunt Marjorie's cottage than he was in fishing. It was only as I grew older that I got my priorities straight.

I couldn't wait, of course, to get my drivers' license just as soon as I turned sixteen. I had passed the test just that afternoon, and was at home in the early evening, proud and impatient to actually be turned free with the car. Dad, as always, was aware of this but subtle. He went to the refrigerator and after looking inside, remarked that we were out of milk. He casually suggested that I might like to run down to the store, in the car, just a few blocks, and get a quart. Might like? I couldn't wait to get behind the wheel of that big Oldsmobile. I had the keys and was out of the house in a flash. Parking in the downtown area of the small town was at an angle toward the curb; I found a space, albeit somewhat narrow, and proudly went into the store for the milk. The problem arose as I backed out of the parking place. Nervous and inexperienced, and unused to the quick acceleration of Dad's big car, I cut the wheels a bit too much as I went into reverse and started to go. The bumper of the old Ford next to me caught under the edge of my front fender and before I could stop it had put tear in the metal, perhaps two inches long. I was sick with dread to tell Dad what had happened, but it was already dark and I knew he had to go into Boston in the morning. I didn't dare tell him, and just hoped he would think someone else had done it. So I just went home with the milk and kept my mouth shut. Two days later Dad told the family that he had noticed an ugly tear in the fender of his car, and said he figured someone had done it in the parking garage in Boston. Just what I had hoped would happen. I was in the clear! All the scrupulously instilled honesty I had grown up with had been ignored, but it had worked. Yet I was troubled by not telling the truth and was tempted many times to confess, but I never did, I just suffered silently.

About three months later Dad had all the numerous dents and scratches repaired on his car. When it was ready I went with him to the local body shop to pick it up. It was beautiful. "Hey Dad," I said "They sure did a great job. The even got the dent out of the back door and the scratches on the trunk."

"Yes," he said, and they fixed the rip you put in the front fender." I had nothing to answer, but it made me realize that my Dad had once been a boy himself, and knew the suffering I had gone through. That was my dad.

It was that year that Dad made a big change. I never knew he was even looking for another job until he announced that he had been asked to take over the advising of the Taiwan Sugar Corporation. He and my mother were to go to Taiwan in just a few months. In the interim he sold his interest in the Frozen Food plant, entered me in a Prep school so I would be at least somewhat supervised, and made arrangement to go on what turned out to eventually be a seven-year assignment. He was in charge, now, of not just one sugar mill but over twenty of them, throughout the island. They returned for vacations a few times during those years, but I was left on my own, with the old house as headquarters and a housekeeper in attendance if I decided to go there. Charlie was in College and he too showed up during vacations and weekends. But we both always worked during summers, and often even during Christmas vacations. We were completely on our own from then on and only really got back with our parents many years later. They returned permanently the year we both were married.

With the selling of the big old family home, they bought a small house on a hilltop on Cape Cod, allowing them to look out to the harbor and the bay, and after a few short consulting jobs in various parts of the world, Dad fully retired. Living modestly but comfortably, Dad bought, in addition to a skiff and small outboard, the inboard cruiser he had always dreamed of. It would sleep two, had a galley and lots of room for fishing. The first two were rarely used but the fishing was frequent.

Dad used to love to tell his story about a time when he went fishing, by himself, on Cape Cod Bay. He shouldn't have been alone, but he was. Evidently none of his usual cronies was available and we two sons were living in other parts of the country, and he wanted to get out on the water. It was a cold and windy day with rough water once he was out of the harbor. So he was wearing, over his undershirt, a woolen long sleeve buttoned shirt and then a pullover sweatshirt. By the time he cleared the outer bar the boat was tossing in the whitecaps and he was considering turning back for home. But he had a line out, from a rod in one of the stern holders and suddenly the reel let out a whine as a fish took the rear three-pronged hook of the blue rebel plug. He slowed the engine, dropped the shift into neutral and staggered back to the rod. Bracing his legs against the transom he worked a good-sized Striped Bass to the boat and guided it around to the port side. How, he wondered, was he going to get it in the boat without falling overboard? He decided to wait for a calm instant, and give a good yank on the leader to quickly get in in, so he could go back to maneuvering the boat. But waves can be deceiving. At what he thought was just the right instant he gave that big yank, but at the same time an unexpected wave helped him mightily. As a result the fish not only came into the boat, but sailed over his head and dropped behind him. On the way down it hit the back of his sweatshirt and the treble hook imbedded itself in his clothing, right in the small of his back, penetrating all three layers of his clothing, yet never touching his skin. Here was a dilemma. He was being tossed about in the middle of the bay with a twelve pound Striper hanging down his back and he couldn't reach the hooks from either above or below, and because of the way the various layers of clothes buttoned and did not button it was not just a question of slipping out of all three. As he told it, every so often the big fish would struggle and slap him on the butt with its tail. Suddenly Dad saw the absurdity and humor in the situation and, alone and befuddled, he started to laugh uproariously. Eventually he worked on the problem, got the sweatshirt over his head and encased the fish in it while he worked on each subsequent laver, until he was cold and shirtless with a fish swathed in his clothes. But he was completely unscathed and he had a nice fish to take home.

That is not to say, though, that he often went fishing, or anywhere else alone. He had a myriad of friends, who would often be involved in any of his projects or activities. Some were fishing buddies and others were clamming buddies. Some picked blueberries and others raked for quahogs at low tide in the salt holes. Moreover, he had an entire set of friends that depended upon him. If he caught fish he would take some to a few retired people who had trouble getting around. If he dug clams they also were distributed, as were berries, and fresh vegetables from his garden. He had one particular friend who was totally blind. Dad would stop by and see him, usually with some groceries, every few days. While there he often read the newspaper to his friend. Dad had many friends, and I never knew of anyone, at any time, anywhere, that disliked my father. I often tried to decide exactly what he had, because I would have liked to be more like him. I believe, looking back, that it was his genuineness. Even as a top person in his profession, he never acted superior to anyone. He was raised with a New England accent, and he never tried to get rid of it. Dad knew nothing of classical music or art, and little about literature except what rubbed off from my very literate mother, and he never pretended he did. With this man what you saw was the real thing, take it or leave it. And everyone he met was anxious to take it.

I think those years on Cape Cod were the happiest of his life. He did not just sit back and do nothing because he was retired. He seemed to have to remain active. He had projects going at all times. Once, running low on new things to do, he took a course at the Community College in re-caning chairs. So did many others, I am sure, and most then moved on to something else. But Dad used it to start a small business. New England antiques were in many homes and a great number of the chairs had seats that were broken through or sagged with age and needed redoing. Before long, just through referrals, he was inundated in work.

It was a few years thereafter that the transition from Dad to Abuelito occurred. When the grandchildren came upon the scene he was delighted. They took priority over anything else, and became his companions in any project he dreamed up. All these years later those three grandchildren still develop faraway looks and a smile when they talk about being at "The Cape" with "Abuelito and Grammy Cape". They recall days at the beach or rides on the ferry to Nantucket. They remember just doing errands with him and they recall when he took them to the small county fair where they could ride the Ferris wheel. They even learned to eat freshly opened clams as they found them and dug them up on the sand flats of the harbor. He was fun because he was as much of a kid as they were. Eventually he had taught my son to catch his first Striper just as he had taught me.

Shortly after they celebrated their fiftieth

wedding anniversary everything changed. I was in New York on business and was just about to go to lunch with some associates when I received a phone call from my brother telling me to get there as soon as possible. "Grammy Cape" had been hospitalized. A helicopter to LaGuardia and a quick trip over the ocean, finally leaving Nantucket, the island of years back, below us like a sandy crescent, and I was soon riding in Charlie's car to the hospital. I hadn't realized how the years had changed us all, with my mother looking pale and yet somehow angelic with her white hair carefully combed by the nurse, creating a misty halo around her head, as she smiled up from the hospital bed. I am sure she was completely aware of the gravity of her condition, yet she was serene. She had always seemed large and hearty, and now she seemed frail and small. It didn't seem possible that I had been too busy to notice the years going by. And Abuelito was suddenly a much older man than we all had realized. The dynamic energy had disappeared and he seemed worn and haggard. I looked about the room and saw that my brother also was older, and realized they must be seeing the same things in me. The years were suddenly gone and the stability was being upset. One of the anchors was disappearing before our eyes.

At my urging Abuelito came to visit us about three months after she died. He and his younger brother drove across the country to New Mexico. Abuelito would stay with us, it was planned, while Uncle Jack would continue on to see relatives in California. They arrived in midafternoon of a cold February day. Dad had always been meticulous in his appearance but now he was wearing a spotted and dirty sweater and wrinkled khaki pants. He even needed a shave which also seemed out of character. But what was most disturbing was his lack of enthusiasm, even on greeting his beloved granddaughter. Broken is too harsh a word, but he was discouraged. It was clear he had lost his enthusiasm for life. Also, something was worrying him. It didn't take long to find out what. He soon announced that he was not feeling well, and wanted to see a doctor. It was clear he had been putting something off and waiting until he could be with us, but now it was time to act. "I'm going to call Doctor Jim." He said. "I want him to come over and take look at me." It was apparent he was in pain, and he said he hurt in his abdomen, but when we suggested going to the Emergency Ward he refused. We tried to explain that doctors did not make house calls any more, but Abuelito knew Jim was only three houses up the street, had seen him in his office for something on a prior visit, and he trusted him. I felt he had been planning this as he and Jack drove across the country, and was not now about to be deterred. We finally gave in and found Jim's home phone number. I don't know what Dad said, but within minutes Jim was at my front door, and within a couple of hours Dad had been transported by ambulance to the hospital and admitted. It had only taken an instant for Jim to see and feel the swelling to know it was an Aortic Aneurism. His Aorta, the main blood conduit below the heart, was swollen up to many times its normal size, and was close to bursting. Two days later he was in nine hours of surgery to replace much of the Aorta.

For three weeks he was in intensive care.

Most of that time he was sedated and made little sense, and much of that time, also, he seemed unlikely to make it. But he was tough old bird and eventually improved enough to be moved out of intensive care. His nurses told me that attending to him was like a travelogue. One day he would be in Cuba, another in Taiwan and next, perhaps, Paraguay. He would be bossing workers in Spanish, Chinese or English, or sometimes in a combination of the three. They said they could ask him where he was and he would tell them. It was many more weeks before he was allowed to come to our home where we cared for him.

One weekend, after months of recuperation we decided it was time for a break, a change of scene. He had regained a great deal of strength, but was obviously bored and depressed. We were hearing constant requests to let him go back to his home on Cape Cod, but it was obvious he was not yet fit to live alone and care for himself, much less drive back alone. He had, in the past, loved our simple log cabin in the San Juan Mountains of Colorado, so we decided to take him there for a few days. He was suddenly animated and happy. Sitting in the front seat beside me as I drove, we talked at great length about the years now gone when we had all been young and healthy.

It is a long drive though, and after a couple of hours of travel and talk we all became quiet and thoughtful. North of the State Line I suddenly had an idea, but said nothing about it. He had, for just short time, been so happy, I wanted to try to prolong it. Looking back , I realize now after many years that I am at just about the same age as he was then. I think I saw that I would be there someday, and realized it was up to me to do something. Without saying anything to anyone I turned left onto a dirt road that led over the steep escarpment of Florida Mesa, and down to the farmlands, meadows and orchards below, cut through the middle by the Animas River. Of course I was asked where I was going and I merely replied, "Wait and see."

Where the steep drop starts to meet the valley there is a spring of cold water. That is, it is cold in the summer but relatively warm in the winter, making it ideal for the growth of trout, year around. The flow is large and dependable, making it perfect for a fish hatchery. And that is what was and still is there, and that is where I was heading. I knew that this privately owned hatchery that supplied trout to restaurants and hatchlings to private waters, also had a large pond full of mature and sometimes trophy-sized rainbows and browns. Moreover, for a price, they would let you fish in that pond. Yes, it was a high price for a trout but I felt we might catch one or two for the next morning's breakfast. I knew Abuelito would love it, and perhaps I could restore the elation of earlier.

I pulled up on the gravel, below the banking that contained the fishing pond and parked beneath a large cottonwood tree. The main hatchery with its tanks of eggs and tiny hatchlings was in front of us. Up the slope beyond the fishpond were other large rectangular ponds, filled with trout. Each pond held only one size of trout, from minnows to eating size. Remember, these trout, including the ones in the special fishing pond had never met a person they did not like. At regular intervals a man would walk out on a platform and throw them buckets of fish food. When those buckets of food splashed into the water a feeding frenzy would immediately occur as each trout rushed to get his share. So if anything that looked at all edible hit the surface of the water the fish would compete to see who would eat it.

After clearing it with the young boy who had been put in charge by his parents, the owners of the hatchery, we went to work getting Abuelito up the grassy banking, he with a cane and one of us on each side of him. A folding chair was positioned for him in the shade of the tree, close to the water. All of my quality fishing gear was at the cabin, of course, so we had to use what the boy presented us with. That turned out to be an antiquated fiberglass rod fitted with a cheap closed-face spin casting reel, and line strong enough to haul in Moby Dick. That didn't seem to worry Dad a bit. He had fished with hand lines on the Paraguay River and he had fished with thousand-dollar reels for Tuna on the Atlantic. He had bottom fished for Cod and fly cast for Steelhead. He knew how to handle them and he could certainly handle this. He was a fisherman, come what may. After the first trial cast that went into the weeds at the far bank, he had a feel for it. The next cast landed at the head of the pool, where the fresh water tumbled in from the spring above. He hardly had time to engage the reel when the first fish hit. My first reaction was to look at the fish as it leaped out of the water. The ugly lure was dangling from his lower jaw and he was a brown trout, a beauty. I was elated, and then I looked over at Abuelito, and received the real reward. He had an immense grin as he cranked on that ancient and clumsy reel. It was the father I remembered all the way from fishing for Tarantulas in Cuba to catching Marlin in Mazatlan. Never mind the surgery or the months of recuperation. He had even put aside his beloved wife's death. He was fishing and that was all that mattered at that instant. He was back on his boat on Cape Cod Bay, or trolling for Barracuda off Venezuela. He was ice fishing in Massachusetts or fly-fishing in Turkey. He worked that fish in as if it had been a trophy Bluefish. As soon it was flopping on the grass and we had removed the hook he was ready to go again. The next cast was taken just as readily and now we had two fish on the grass.

By now I was a bit apprehensive. Any fish landed had to be kept, by the rules of the hatchery. No catch and release was allowed, regardless of the size of the fish. Moreover, they were charging us by the inch of fish caught. We already had close to forty inches of fish on the grass. The lures had big sharp hooks with barbs. Unlike a barbless hook, there was little chance of shaking off a less desirable catch. Mentally I was already calculating the cash in my pocket versus the fish on the grass. Then I looked again at my father. He had no idea that these fish were expensive. But he was the happiest I had seen him in many months. "Hell, I have my checkbook in the glove box! This man deserves everything I can give him. He certainly has given me everything he could over all these years. Now it's my turn."

After a number of other fish, all edible also, I reminded myself, Dad got tired. "I guess we should leave some for the next guy." He said. He would not ever admit that he was too tired to continue fishing. So we picked up his fish, asked the boy to clean them for us, also at a price of course, and helped Dad back down the grassy slope and into the car. After I went up to the office to pay the bill I came back and saw that he was still sitting, just as I had left him, and he still had a foolish grin.

Dad lived a number of years after that, but I want to always remember him as he sat by that pond that day.

THE PERFECT JOB

Mr. Chase lived next door. Not only that, he was the father of my best friend. His son was known as Frankie in those days, and adults called Mr. Chase, Frank, but even many years later when I was a married man with my own children he was still Mr. Chase to me. I would not have thought to call him anything else. When I was a boy he had a garage, a building beside and somewhat behind his shingle-sided house in that small New England town. On the front of that garage, over the single door, was a large weathered, hand painted sign that read "BOATS...ROW...MOTOR...SAIL" in large letters. And if you wanted a perfect job on the building of a boat, Mr. Chase could do it.

As his sign said, it could be any type of boat, as long as it would fit in his garage, and he would craft a minor masterpiece. Perfection in boats mattered to Mr. Chase. Not just in his boats, but in the use of his boats. It was from him that I learned the nuances of fishing on Buzzards Bay.

But that perfectionism was a burden for Frankie and me. We would go fishing with our two fathers, and fishing with them called for doing things right. Particularly I recall being told so many times I could anticipate the next time I would hear it, that you could not catch a fish if the bait had weeds on it. That was the command that indicated it was time to reel in the long lines being dragged behind the boat and check for seaweed that might have been picked up as we trolled. Of course often he was right, there would be a gob of weeks snarled in the hook, but sometimes he was wrong. But fishing, to him, was not sitting back, huddled against the early morning cold, just holding the rod. Fishing successfully involved work. And it was work that he expected. I sometimes wondered why the boat even had holders built into the transom. We were not allowed to just leave a rod there, waiting for a bite. It was mandatory that the rod be held and moved at all times. We were required to constantly move the rod tip forward and backward, adding more action to the smooth running bait. Usually what we were trolling was a lead-headed nylon buck tail or a feather lure, with either a sea worm or a strip of squid fluttering from the bend of the hook. Supposedly the constant pumping on the rod elicited more bites and therefore more fish. I would not have dared to audibly question the theory, but under my breath I did a great deal of mumbling. In retrospect, I know he was right, but I also think that it was part of his philosophy that dictated the work. Any fishing had to be done with perfection, and it was time two adolescent boys learned that. So pump we did, and check for weeds we did, over and over and over. We started as the first light was just spreading over the bay, and we kept it up until the hot sun had us shedding our sweatshirts, and we were still pumping those rods until it was time to head for home late in the afternoon. But once in a while we would be rewarded with a hit from a Striper or Bluefish. Then the instruction really kicked in. "Hold that rod tip up! Don't stop reeling. Keep a tight line. Come on, get him in, we need to go back through that spot and get another one. Don't reel past the swivel! Hold on while I gaff him." It was even more difficult if there were other boats near us. He did not want them to see we were catching fish or they might encroach on our territory, so in addition to trying to land the fish we were told to pretend we did not have fish on. It was demanding, but we loved the sport and we learned from the expert.

Mr. Chase did not just become a fisherman, he was, I believe, born into it. He was a Cape Codder and his ancestors before him were Cape Codders. Yet he did not inherit some of the personality traits we associate with the breed. Yes, he could be stern and often he had little to say, but he also had an astonishing sense of humor and could be extremely outgoing. I contrast him to his Father, who was an old man when I was a boy, but I got to know when he came to live with Frankie's family. Saying I got to know him may be an exaggeration, however. Pa Chase, as everyone called him, was as taciturn as any man I ever met. With effort it might be possible to elicit a single word answer from him. He was from Harwich, about half way between the Cape Cod Canal and Provincetown at the far end. To Pa Chase if you lived on the mainland side of the canal you were a foreigner. In fact if you were nearer the canal than Harwich you were a bit suspect. I never learned much about Pa Chase, because he said so little. His main amusement was to take the bus, nearly daily, to the nearest large town, where there were movie theaters, and see every new movie. But it was under his influence that Mr. Chase had learned the ways of being a Cape Codder, including fishing. So it was surprising that the son was not more like his Father. I remember Pa Chase as small man. Mr. Chase was a large and heavyset man with dark hair, in those days, and a smile that was overwhelming. In my mind today I can still hear his laugh. He liked beer, but rarely took anything stronger, and he loved a good cigar. He liked steak, rare. But his passion was fishing. Mr. Chase did not play golf or tennis. He had no use for bowling. But in winter he built boats and he went ice fishing in order to amuse himself until the fish showed up on Buzzards Bay. Of course boat building was not his sole work; he was a responsible family man and a hard worker. The boat building was sporadic and more recreational than remunerative, I believe. But when he built one it became a great pleasure and a demanding pursuit in which nothing was ever done half way. When into a boat building project the light was on late at night in that garage, and it occupied most of his extra time. But on Sunday mornings when the rest of his family were at church he often would be at home, sitting in front of the small round screen of the TV of his day and watch a fishing program. Perhaps he was also in his church.

Many years later, when I was a college student and Frankie was flying helicopters for the Air Force, I was home for a weekend and Mr. Chase, now an older man with more of a pot belly, but still strong and active and still a determined fisherman, asked me if I would like to go fishing with him on Saturday. I was pleased at the honor, and accepted with enthusiasm. I found to my delight that it was still a routine that had never changed. I met him with my car, packed with rods, foul weather gear, boxes of lures, leaders and hooks, and with some sandwiches and cold drinks, at the usual extremely early hour of the morning. After a long drive through almost deserted roads, and then onto the main road to The Cape we stopped, as we always had, at the same café, or one very much the same, because I felt I recognized the two sleepy customers at the counter and the tee-shirted cook behind the small serving window who cooked our bacon and eggs and then brought them around to us. The coffee was no better now than it had been years before, probably left over from the prior evening and still being reduced to a bitter sludge. Yet I reveled in the feeling of repetition and nostalgia. Later we stopped once more, at the same bait shop for squid and sea worms, and before sunup we were motoring carefully and slowly away from Wareham and toward the West end of the canal. From this distant point my memory does not let me remember if we caught anything, or if so what or how many, but I recall vividly that we fished in all the places I remembered. We worked along the Sand Spit, which always had seemed a misnomer to me since it was rock not sand. Then we fished the entrance to the canal and later, as I recall, we went across to the other side and fished off Wings Neck. Certainly there was more but I particularly recall those names and places. They were an echo of my childhood, and the finest part was that I was with Mr. Chase. And, moreover, he didn't have to chide me for not keeping the rod tip moving.

It was not very long thereafter that Mr. Chase's perfectionism in fishing came to fruition. His many years of selling the fish he caught to the local markets had not gone unnoticed. Also, other regulars on the water had gotten to know his boats over the years and many had taken to following him when he went out, to find out where the fishing was likely to be good. He had rightfully acquired the reputation as a man who knew his fishing, and particularly as a man who knew those waters in all seasons and all tidal and weather conditions. He had acquired the reputation as one of the best.

While Mr. Chase was acquiring the reputation as an expert fisherman, another man, expert in his own field, and unknown to Mr. Chase, had reached the realization that he was not, himself, a great fisherman, but he loved fishing. In fact, he had even bought a large vacation home, not far from the water in that same area of Cape Cod. He was a very successful and well-known Judge, and was not lacking in money. But a Striped Bass does not hold a fisherman in high esteem just because he has money. That is the wonderful thing about fishing. It is the great leveler. It does not matter if you approach the trout stream afoot or in a Rolls Royce. It doesn't matter if rod is split bamboo from London or a tree branch with a piece of string. The boat can be a yacht or a rowboat, and still some people catch fish and some don't. The equipment helps, but it is the person handling the equipment that makes the difference. The Judge knew how to read the law, but he did not know how to read the state of the tide and the direction of the wind. He could put a man behind bars more easily than he could put a fish on ice

If you could have asked Mr. Chase what his perfect job would be he might have told you that it would be to do nothing but fish and build and work on boats. All day, every day. If you had been able to ask the Judge what his ideal relaxation would be he might have told you he would want to be able to go fishing and catch fish. All day, any day. That is, any day he was able to get away from his demanding duties.

They met one day in late September. The Judge had made inquiries and knew what he was looking for. Soon the search narrowed down to one man, repeatedly mentioned, by the name of Chase. A phone call and a meeting ensued. The Judge had spent a lifetime assessing men. He could spot honesty or dishonesty with great speed. He disliked, more than anything, pretense. He respected hard work and he always was on the lookout for true expertise. The man he met with passed the test with flying colors. It was already too late in the season to try to do what he had in mind that year, but he also realized that he did not want to lose this man. In addition, he needed a better boat. So the verdict was reached and the sentence was handed down; the offer was made, and accepted. Mr. Chase was to go on the payroll immediately. His duties for the winter were to build a boat for the Judge. It was to be a boat that suited Mr. Chase. It had to be the perfect fishing boat for those waters. Not too big for easy maneuvering in the tricky rips and winds of Buzzards Bay, nor too small for the comfort of up to four people. But mostly it was to be a boat specifically intended for fishing. It did not need to be beautiful, just practical. The Judge would not interfere in any way with the choices made in the design and construction of the boat. He would just pay the bills. As early in the spring as was possible, the duties would change. After launching, testing, equipping and adjusting the boat, it was to be made ready so that any time, with little or no advanced notice, the Judge could show up, with or without companions, to go fishing and it would be ready to go. From then on it was Mr. Chase's job to know where the fish were and what they were biting on. The Judge was wise enough to know that fish moved around with changes in weather , tides and water temperature. Also, they fed on different smaller fish at different times and in different places. Moreover, he knew they were very changeable and very unpredictable. The only way to know all these things was to go fishing. In fact, the more one fished the better he became at guessing where they would be and what they would be eating. So the job required that Mr. Chase fish every day. Yes, every day, without fail, regardless of weather and without interruption. The Judge wanted to be sure that whenever he suddenly decided he could get away for a day or two the odds of catching fish had been swung in his favor. So he was willing to pay an expert to do just that. Mr. Chase Had landed the perfect job for a fisherman, and the Judge thereafter landed   a   lot   more   fish.

THE CATCHER ON THE ICE

In case you live in some one of those other states, like Minnesota or Washington or somewhere, with different laws, let me tell you that Massachusetts has some pretty funny ways of letting you fish. Like, in the summer you can fish with two lines but in the winter you can fish with five. Tell me, who the hell is going to fish with two lines in the summer when it takes two hands to use one pole. But in the winter when all you want to do is keep warm and sit still by a fire they tell you you need to have five lines. I tell you, those must be a bunch of jerks or phonies that make those laws. I bet you most of them have never even been ice fishing. In fact they probably none of them have ever been fishing

at all. At least not like I have with my Dad.
Not that I don't like to go fishing with my
dad. I do. And I even like to go ice fishing
with him even if you do freeze your ass off
and all. One thing I like is that my Dad takes
me fishing and all, not like a bunch of kids I
go to school with hardly ever see their dad,
either because he is always too busy or maybe
because their parents are divorced and his
mother has custody or something. But my
dad knocks me out, he really does. My Dad is
a real unusual kind of man. He never does
what a kid thinks his dad should do, but its
funny how lots of times he seems to be right.

It's like the time, back when I was just a kid,
and me and Dad, we were going to go ice
fishing one Saturday. There's this big lake just
about a million miles away, and it's a real good
ice fishing lake. It has a gazillion islands so
you can go out there and set yourself up a fire
and all, and then put out your fishing tilts and
sit on land and watch for the fish to bite. Oh
yeah, so tilts, for you that don't know about it,
are these like crosses of wood that you put
over the hole you cut in the ice. Then they
have a reel that goes under water so it won't

freeze and a red flag that springs up when some dumb fish that forgot to hibernate tries to take your minnow and gets hooked instead. It drives me nuts to see these guys in the movies, like in that movie that was called "Grumpy Old Men", I think it was, that sit on their asses in a little shack out on the ice and dangle a single line in the water. Like some dumb fish is going to come along and not see this asshole looking down right over him. I don't see how they ever get anything except a damned cold. At least we have the brains to sit by a warm fire on shore, and drink coffee or hot chocolate or something and don't have to be sitting on the damned ice. Some people don't have enough brains to not sit on the ice when they could be drinking hot chocolate.

So we put all this stuff together and pile it in the trunk of this old clunker of a Chevy. It's a lot of crap you have to take for ice fishing. We have this, like, box on a sled, with a rope so you can pull it over the lake to where you're going. In it we had ten of these tilts. Like I said, the crumby laws say you can have five for each guy. They fold up kind of, so you can cram a lot of them in the box together. Then you got to have an ice chisel to cut the holes. It's like a great big sharp squared-off blade welded to the end of a pipe, and it's got a leather wrist strap. That's because some kid is likely to not have a good hold on the pipe when he's holding it with his mittens on, and it goes down through the ice and to the bottom of the lake. I never did that but one of my friends Kenny, did once, so my dad wants to be careful. He was a kind of a dumb kid, Kenny was, but I kind of liked him anyway. Except he was always saying things like "When are we going home?" or something. I hate it when kids say dumb things like "When are we going home?" If he wanted to stay home why did he go anyway and then bother everybody by wishing he was home. But where was I? Oh yeah, so we take the ice chisel and then we got to have a skimmer to take the ice out of the hole we just made and to keep off the ice when it starts to refreeze around our tilts. Oh yeah, and there's this tackle box with a bunch of hooks and stuff and then the bait bucket with about ten million minnows we bought swimming around in it. Only every so often a bunch of them just go belly up and die so we have to scoop them out and throw them out on the ice where they can freeze solid. But, anyhow, when they are dead we can't use them for bait. In fact, when they stop swimming real friskily we usually shake them off the hook and put on a new one anyway. That's why we have to have so many. It kind of seems funny, like we're trading about a million little fish for every big one we catch. Oh yeah, and we take, like you could figure, some sandwiches and some hot drinks in thermoses, so when the fishing gets quiet we can warm ourselves up.

So this one time we get up real early like my dad likes to do, and we drive to the lake I was telling about. When we get there it's still colder than hell, because the sun is just like coming up, and we have all these coats and hats and mittens and everything on and we are still freezing our asses off, and we take this sled out of the back of the car and we hike about a jillion miles on the ice to this little damned island. We hiked by a bunch of other islands but only this particular one would do. But one good thing was, by the time we got there we had worked up a sweat and we weren't like blocks of ice anymore. One thing I don't like is freezing. Some people, like this friend of mine in school, Freddie McGowan, likes to act like a goddam athlete or something and run around in like a tee-shirt or something in the snow. I sure hate it when people run around in the snow like it was summer. I really do.

When we got to where my Dad wanted to go, we left our thermoses and lunch and stuff there to kind of put dibs on where we wanted to sit on the shore and went out to dig the holes in the ice. They got to be, you know, like about a foot across. Too much and the tilt won't fit and too small and it's too hard to do the catching. That is, if you ever do the catching, which is damned seldom in my opinion. But still I like to go because for one thing I am with my Dad, and because I do like to fish, I really do. Of course that isn't to say the hole has to be that big to get the fish through it. Hell no. Those fish are just little perch or pickerel. I guess the bass and all are probably sleeping and can't be bothered looking for our little minnows when the water is so damned cold. It takes some dumb little perch or something to be nosing around underneath that like six inches of ice. That kills me!

But when we got out there and started to figure out where we wanted to put our ten lines, you know what, someone had already cut holes just about where we wanted them, except they were kind of frozen in. The ice wasn't thick like the lake in general, but we had to still cut it with the ice chisel. It was like someone had been fishing there before us, maybe the day before of something, Dad had me do some hole cutting and I just about forgot to put the strap around my wrist, but then I remembered before my Dad could remind me. I sure didn't want to be dumb like Kenny. We had the sled with us, with the bait bucket and tilts and all so after we cut each hole we put in a tilt, put a minnow on the hook, with it just through the skin of its back so as not to kill it but to hold it on the hook. You got to be really careful when you do that. I learned when I was just a little kid to do it, so I could do it really well and Dad trusted me to bait the hooks right. I hate it when some kid doesn't know how to do it right. If some kid doesn't put the minnow on right it won't swim natural, and no self-respecting pickerel of perch will want to eat it.

Once we had all them damned tilts out there, baited and ready to catch a million fish, we went back in to the place we had picked out, where we could see all the tilts and spot any time a red flag went up. Someone had already had a fire there, because there was a ring of rocks and some dead black logs in the middle. There was even a couple of big logs pulled over near the fireplace, so you could sit there and keep warm and still watch for those red flags. Boy, I tell you, you really have to keep your eye out, because if you don't pay attention and see when a flag starts going you don't get there in time and then you never catch the fish. Here is what my Dad taught me you got to do. As soon as you see a red flag you hurry out across the ice, but trying not to make too much noise to scare every goddamned fish in the lake away. When you get there you quickly lift the tilt out of the hole and grab the line real lightly between your thumb and finger. That means you got to take off your gloves or mittens, which is no fun, believe me, and grab that icy line, but that is what you have to do. If you didn't take too damned long getting there the line will be slipping out between your fingers from the fish swimming away with the bait, you know. But then this is the tricky part. Pretty quick the fish will stop going away from you. My Dad says that the fish stops to turn the minnow around in his mouth to swallow it. I don't know how he knows that, and maybe it's just a theory, but anyway, the fish just kind of stops. That's when you have to just wait a second and then give a quick yank to set the hook, but not too hard to pull it out of his mouth, and then you just haul the fish in hand over hand, still freezing your fingers but it's fun anyway. If it works you got a fish out flopping on the ice next to the hole. My dad always gets the fish off the hook then, because one time I was doing it, and I kind of wasn't paying attention and the fish just flipped right back into the hole and went home. But that was when I was a dumb little kid, but he still doesn't want me doing it.

So this one day, like I was telling you, we

get it all set up and then we go on the little damned island and sit on the cold logs, and start to freeze our asses for real. "Ah." My dad says. "This is the life." He acts like it's a summer day and he's sitting under a tree drinking lemonade, for god sake. But you know, it really was pretty nice, even if it was cold as a witch's tit. So he gets out my hot chocolate and his coffee that he fixes with lots of cream and sugar and we watch for red flags. And, believe it or not, we hardly got a gulp down when we had two flags go up, just about at the same time. So I went for the close one, like he told me, and he made for the one further out. When I got there the line was still going out, and I guess I did everything right for a change, because when he stopped running I had my mittens off and was ready and before that fish knew it I had him out on the ice. And then, because my dad was busy I took him off the hook and I didn't let him flip back in the lake. He was a pickerel that is like, if you don't know, kind of a small long fish with big teeth, like a pike only not so big. Some people like to eat them, like my mom for instance, but they are loaded with a jillion tiny bones that make them no fun to eat. But we take them home and my parents eat them anyway.

I got back to the fire first, because, believe me, my goddam hands were freezing and I had to carry that fish back in my bare hands so it wouldn't slip. I didn't even want to eat it but I had to take it back anyway. But I was really kind of proud of that fish, it being bigger than the usual ones, and I wanted to show it to Dad. And when he got back he hadn't gotten his. But you wouldn't have known it the way he said all about what a good fish I had caught, and how it would be great for my mother when we got back. I mean, my dad was a good sport and didn't let it show, but I know he probably didn't like not getting his.

That was all the fishing we got for a while and we are just sitting there, kind of sleepy from having got up so early and all, and hardly noticed anything anywhere else until dad kind of motioned to me and pointed down the ice, back in the direction of where we left the car. Then is when began what I started to tell you about; the interesting part. Way down there I see a dot, then it becomes two together, coming toward us. Getting closer I see its two people pulling a sled, kind of like ours over the ice and all rolled up in lots of warm clothes. It was a big man and a woman who might not have looked so short and fat except for all the coats and sweaters and scarfs and a million things she had on to keep warm. The guy was real old, probably fifty or sixty or something, because he had lots of grey hair sticking out from under this red hunting cap. You know, the checkered kind with ear flaps that, of course, he had down over those big ears I could even see because they were so big. He had on these padded khaki type pants and rubber boots, just like mine and Dad's, so I knew he must be an ice fisherman too. His face was real red like he was working hard to pull that little sled, which was no more than the one I had pulled for us, and I didn't get all winded and everything. I sure wouldn't have picked that woman with him for a girlfriend but I guess he did, because I could tell for sure they were not married. I mean, he was walking close to her, not ahead of her, and they were looking at each other once in a while that isn't typical if you know what I mean. Not that she was ugly or anything, just that in all those clothes she looked like a big teddy bear with a hat that was tied around over her ears and pulled down over her forehead. Maybe under it all she was okay.

They were headed right for us, and the guy looked real stern and unhappy. "What are you doing in my fishing place?" I could see he was kind of showing off for his girlfriend because of the way he glanced over at her to see her reaction. Boy what a jerk. I mean, the least he could do was say hello and how's the fishing and all before he acted like such an asshole. It kills me how some guy can act that way just for some girlfriend he takes to a goddam lake to go ice fishing. That rally knocks me out, let me tell you.

"I didn't see your name on it." Says my dad, calm as can be. He can sometimes be calm like that but I learned long ago to watch out when he is because maybe underneath he is boiling. I've seen it before. But this jerk didn't know my dad like I do. I guess he was looking for a reaction and he didn't get it. Not that I am saying my dad would ever have been real mean to me, but I sure knew when we had gotten to a point where I had better stop talking. But this gorilla didn't know him like I do. "I guess you didn't get up early enough this morning. It seems to me this is a public lake, and we have fishing licenses." Says Dad.

The big guy took off his hat and shook out his grey hair that looked like he needed a haircut pretty bad. "I fish here every day. Those holes you are using are the ones I put in there. Only reason I'm late is my lady friend here had to pretty herself up for the fish. So, if you don't mind, Pal, why don't you and your boy find another place to fish?" I could see he really was putting on an act for her now. He was a big guy, and had a face that looked like maybe he had once been a boxer or something. I mean, his nose was kind of flattened and sideways and he had these big cauliflower ears I told you about. But he had a big belly and didn't look to be in great shape. And let me tell you, my dad isn't a little guy either and he stays in good shape even though he spends most of his time in an office. He used to play football in college, and I bet he could have gone on to the pros if he had wanted to. I figured Dad could take him easy. In fact, if you want to know the truth, I wanted to see my dad punch his lights out. Not that I had even seen my dad punch anybody, but I knew he could if he wanted to, and this guy was really asking for it. "Look Pal," he went on, "Technically I was here first. Yesterday and the day before and even last week." Did you ever notice people never say Pal to somebody that really is their pal? They say it to sound mean and sarcastic. But he was really laying on the tough guy routine for his teddy bear.

Boy, I just was waiting for the explosion. But then came the funny part. Dad, staying just as cool, says, "Look pal," giving it right back to him, "My son and I came out here on a beautiful Saturday for a nice day of fishing. I know that is why you two are here too. And there are lots of fish in there for all of us. I have a warm fire over there, and even a little rum tucked away in my box. Those logs you probably pulled up to the fire yourself, seat four. I suggest we share the area. If you and I were to go out with our two ice chisels we could cut another ten holes in no time, putting some out to the left and others over there beyond my close ones."

"Yeah?" And you would get my old holes where I always get the good fish, right?"

"Hell no, but I won't turn them all over to you, either. Hey, were fishermen, right? The fun is in the fishing, and part of fishing is being with other people when we do it. Lets' just draw straws for who goes in what order and then any flag that goes up is for the next guy."

So what could this poor guy do? If he still tries to start a fight his girlfriend is going to see that he really is an asshole. But this way he can kind of look like he is winning. My dad should have been a diplomat or something. He had that guy in a corner and liking it. But I still might have liked to see Dad flatten his nose even further and I bet he could have done it, too.

"Hey, maybe you got something there. I even have a touch of brandy in my box, and maybe more fried chicken than we need. The name is Al and this here is Jeanie. Hey boy. You like to fish?" Do I like to fish he asks me, like if not what the hell am I doing out there on that goddam cold frozen lake? Sometimes when guys like this Al are talking to young guys like me they treat us like little kids. It drives me crazy. But I tell him yes, I like to fish.

Next thing I know me and this Jeanie are sitting by the fire and she turns out to be kind of nice in an old sort of way, and Dad and this Al guy are out there chopping more holes in the ice. She and I talk and she doesn't treat me like a kid either. Like, old people are always wanting to know what grade you are in, like you are still in kindergarten or elementary or something. She tells me I don't have to call her Miss something-or-other but just to call her Jeanie. But this Jeanie and I talk about how great my dad is and how she hopes Al will be a nice guy now. She even kind of tells me her life history and I tell her a little about myself. I almost didn't want the fish to start biting right then or anything, and they didn't.

So after a while Dad and Al come back and they are acting like old buddies. They are laughing and telling fishing stories. They even find they know some of the same people. And just like Dad had said, we drew straws to see who would go first and second and all, and then we went by it. It helped, and I think maybe Dad, who had the straws, fixed it so Al went first. Later he even got the biggest fish of the day. Once in a while Dad or Al would go over, pull a small bottle from the box and they would each take swig. Not much, you know, and when it was just Dad and me he never pulled out that bottle, but we both knew it was there. But I guess it mellowed Al. Jeanie was offered some but she turned it down, and nobody offered any to me, or I bet I would have taken a big swig.

In the middle of the afternoon we all said we had to get home and we packed up the gear, working together, and pulled the two sleds back to our cars, still with Al and Dad talking and Jeanie and me behind them walking together pulling the sleds. And, will you believe it, when we got back to the cars we decided to get together the next weekend and do it again! My dad should have been working for the government or something, arranging peace treaties. He knocks me out, he really does!

TURN OF THE TIDE

"God … damn! God … damn! God… damn!" He repeated it on each stroke like a cadence, with each arm-wrenching pull of the oars. Lean forward on "God" and backward on "damn"; a steady rhythm swearing the heavy skiff through the water. The object of the boy's wrath was apparent. Every time he leaned forward and adjusted his blistered hands on the cracked wooden handles of the sun-dried oars and raised the oar blades with a twist of his wrist preparing for another painful pull it was there, just two feet in front of his hands, the hated, silent, and useless antiquated and low powered outboard motor. It was, as he knew too well, a cold piece of dead metal. It had pretty chrome trim and a shiny blue highly lustrous case, but inside it was a piece of temperamental steel with a perverse desire to complicate his pleasure. It was heavy and cold and evil. It always ran well inside the harbor. It was the picture of reliability when the sun was shining, the tide was running and the water was mirror smooth. It seemed to know just when it was far enough from shore, when the tide was running against it, when the whitecaps were starting to build and the wind was slopping water over the bow that it was time to become problematical. It would cough and sputter and seemed to slow and then race erratically, it would stop and start and demand attention. He and his father would need to attend to the belligerent outboard and nurse it along, sometimes slowly and sometimes at full throttle, to keep it working. It was always when there were fish jumping and gulls diving in all directions that the spark plug would somehow become fouled, necessitating taking it out ,drying it off, wiping it clean and reinserting it. It always ran out of gas when it was nearly impossible to fill the tank on the back of the motor without slopping much of the fuel into the bay because of the tossing waves. And now it hung uselessly on the transom of the skiff refusing to run, no matter how many times they yanked on the starter cord.

His feet were cold. His sneakers, recently new, recently white and fashionable among his friends, rested in three inches or oily and smelly seawater. A rusty coffee can sloshed in the bilge and knocked occasionally against his ankle. The can was always in the skiff to bail out seawater when it sloshed over the bow, the low side or the transom, which was often. Even now, with the following sea, a larger wave would occasionally crest above the transom, slosh over the space on the two sides of the useless motor and add to the load he was forcing through the waters of the harbor. Not only is it useless, he thought, but it makes my job just that much worse. If it were not for the damned motor there would not be so much weight in the stern and the waves from the following sea, wind and tide wouldn't slosh into the boat. Maybe I should throw the son of a bitch overboard.

"Pull a bit on the left oar, Billy" said the

voice from behind him. His father was hunched forward on the bow seat, where he sat facing toward their destination and giving instructions. "That's it, hold her on that course now. If you line up a mark on Sandy Neck and keep it right in line with the engine you should be able to stay on target, even with the sideways push from the tide."

"I know, Dad. I can do it okay. Don't worry about me, just take care of yourself. Why don't you lie down across the seat? Put some of the foul weather gear over you to keep warm. One of the life preservers will work for a pillow. Just try to take it easy until we get in. It isn't much further now."

"I'm okay."

"Sure." he said, trying not to show either the fear or the weariness in his voice. It was still a long way to go. Luckily the coming tide and wind were now with him. Just lean back, he thought, and try not to think about his father. It felt as though he had been pulling on those oars forever. His eyes were blurred and he felt light headed, but he bent forward into the next stroke.

The sun was dropping toward the low

outline of the strip of sand dunes and beach grass called Sandy Neck which separated Barnstable Harbor from Cape Cod Bay. By the time they got back to Scudder Landing it would be getting dark, Billy thought. He had wanted to pull into the commercial landing further down the harbor, but his father had insisted that he was all right, and that they must take the boat back to Scudder Landing where their car was parked. Billy looked down at his hands and saw that the blisters had broken on both of them and that there was blood staining the handles of the oars.

Was it just this morning, he thought, that they had left home to go to The Cape to go fishing? It seemed so long ago that his father had come in to wake him at 2:30 and tell him it was time to go. But he had already been awake. He had slept very little, being so excited, looking forward to the trip. They had loaded the car the night before, with the long rods with their butts on the floor of the front seat and the tips bent against the inside of the roof of the sedan. They were already rigged with their heavy braided green line and wire leaders connected to bronze swivels. The

outboard motor and gasoline can had gone
into the trunk, along with the rusty green
tackle box and the red cooler holding their
sandwiches wrapped in wax paper and their
cold drinks. The car had smelled like a fishing
trip. There was the musty smell of woolen
sweaters which had gotten soaked in salt
water on previous trips and then dried, stiff
and wrinkled. The tackle box still gave off the
aroma of the live many-legged sea worms in
wet seaweed, packed in white cardboard
boxes like the ones you got Chow Mein in at
the Chinese take-out. The foul weather gear
had its own smell of plastic and the boots
gave off the pungent smell of warm rubber.
Over it all was the smell of fish. The tiny
mackerel scales on the tackle box , the smear
of blood dried on the gaff and the smears of
fish oil on the cork grips of the rods carried
their own story. They were perfume to the
boy.

"Dad, how about letting me drive?" Billy
had gotten his "learner permit" just that week,
having turned fifteen a few weeks before.
"That way I can get some practice."

"No, I don't think you're ready. I know you

have had some lessons, but these are twisty country roads and its night. I'll drive tonight. I'll let you drive when I think you are ready."

"Oh, all right. But I could do it. Did you call down to Jack's Bait Shop to find out how the fishing is?"

"No, we can check in with them on the way down. We need some squid for bait anyway."

They passed through a number of small towns with hardly a light showing any of the houses. In one larger town the only traffic light, where the two principle streets crossed, turned red, and they felt foolish stopping and waiting for non-existent traffic. As they circled the town square of another settlement they saw a police car parked on the far side with the drowsy officer leaning forward with his elbows on the steering wheel. The warmth of the car and the steady hum of the engine made Billy feel sleepy. He slumped in the seat, avoiding the fishing rods which angled over his shoulder. In the glow of the dash lights his father's face looked strong and determined. I wonder when he will think I am ready, he thought. Not just to drive, but everything.

They stopped for breakfast at a café in Wareham. The two of them, sitting up at the counter, were the only customers at that early hour. His father ate ham and eggs with coffee. He had eaten a hamburger. The patty was made by hand, not stamped out like a disk of cardboard, and the bun had been toasted on the grill so that the surface shone deliciously in the light over the counter. A half hour later they were at Jack's Bait Shop. There were a number of other fishermen there, bundled up in heavy sweaters and stocking caps, buying leaders and plugs and live bait. They talked about where the fish had been hitting recently. He felt himself a part of a special society.

"There was a bunch of big stripers off the tip of the sand spit on the top of the tide yesterday" said one. "I picked up three on an eel skin rig. Ran about twelve pounds each."

"Yeah. Well I was down at the west end of the canal, right under the railroad bridge casting from the rip-rap and hooked a really big one. He hit on a blue Rebel plug, straightened the hooks and said bye-bye."

"The big one that got away? Heard that

before."

A bearded grey haired man entered the conversation. "I heard the blues have been running on the north side"

"North side?" Billy thought aloud. That was just where they were headed! Maybe they would run into schools of bluefish. They weren't usually as big as stripers but they fought better. "Dad, did you hear that?"

It had still been dark when they had parked above the high water line at the beach called Scudder's. They had worked together to locate, right and drag their boat down to the water. He could tell by the wet sand that it was near high tide but on the ebb. His father had carried the heavy outboard down and tightened it onto the transom while he had carried the rods, tackle box and cooler and all the odds and ends of clothing and tools, and stowed them aboard the little boat. Then, pushing off with the oars, they had tilted the motor into the water, and it had started on the first pull. Its steady throb took them slowly toward the mouth of the harbor, aided by the running tide. The darkness was quickly lifting and they could soon see the cottages on the tip of Sandy Neck. After putting on white feather jigs on both lines, each with a strip of squid like a small pennant trailing on the bend of the steel hook they let out about thirty yards of line over the stern and trolled slowly. Then they poured still hot coffee from the thermos into tin cups, sweet with sugar and whitened with cream, and sat back waiting. The outboard dutifully moved them up and down the channel off the point, dragging the lures through the deep water.

The going tide was soon uncovering the highest parts of the sand bars up harbor and the fast running ebb swirled through the channel. The red nun buoy off the point was swaying and twisting like a horse bucking away from its tether, pulled nearly horizontal by the current so that the white number three painted on its side was awash.

After a fruitless hour of trolling back and forth, first creeping forward against the current and then rushing back with the flow, Billy had looked up overhead and seen a dozen gulls flying high and heading east. "Dad. Look! A bunch of gulls going up; harbor. Maybe they are following fish.

Should we pull in the lines and see where they are going?

"No, look closer. Those are the big grey gulls. With the tide dropping they are going up to feed on crabs and shellfish. Don't pay attention to the grey gulls, they would rather pick up food than dive for it. Besides, with the going tide the fish will be moving out of the harbor not into it. If you want to find fish watch the small white terns not the big grey gulls."

"Like those, out that way?"

"Yes, watch them. The big gulls were flying high so they were on their way somewhere. These are low over the water. They aren't diving, but they see something in the water below them. It's either baitfish that are too deep for them to dive for or big fish that are not feeding, but might. Look how they are moving out with the tide. There, one dived but he didn't come up with anything. But he was after something. Let's bring in the lines and follow them."

"Look Dad! They are bunching up over a spot and starting to dive. Not just here, there's another bunch further out doing the same thing and some others starting to dive in the deep water off the outer bar. Not a big bunch but just little groups, and they are moving fast. Is that Stripers?"

"No, Bluefish... Striped Bass work in bigger bunches, but these are spotty and moving fast, like Blues. Get that line I, we're going fishing!"

By the time they reached the spot where they had seen the first terns diving the birds had flown off, and could be seen diving at another place further offshore. But the sea where they had been feeding had an oily slick and there were small pieces of sand eels floating on the surface.

"That's Blues alright." His father had said. "Look at the mess they left behind. They tear through a school of baitfish like a threshing machine. The sand eels don't stand a chance with the fish coming up under them and the terns diving down from above. We were too late for this bunch but they will surface again nearby and pretty soon. Rig your line with a yellow nylon jig and I'll use a blue one. Keep them in the water and if we spot a close school we'll get to it in a hurry."

The next time the fish started to feed they were close by. His father was careful to circle the school rather than cut across it. That way they wouldn't spook the fish, and the lures, making a smaller circle than the boat, dragged through the midst of the feeding frenzy. Then he hooked his first Blue. The savage strike stripped a lot of line off his reel before he tightened down on the drag. It was suddenly as tight as a guitar string and he was afraid the rod would be pulled out of his hands. So as to not have the line break he eased off a bit on the drag, grudgingly giving line to the fish when it lunged. His shoulders ached by the time he was able to bring the fish in close to the side of the skiff so his father could gaff it and lift it into the boat, where, even there, the fish was snapping its jaws at anything in reach. It was almost a disappointment to see the size of the fish. It had fought harder than any Striper he had ever caught, yet it was only about five pounds.

The next time the fish showed they were further out to sea. They hurried to them and his father worked in a somewhat smaller fish. A flock of working birds showed further out and they dashed toward it, arriving too late. Then another flock to the north and then one to the east. By the time they had brought in five fish, shuddering and slapping on the slats at the bottom of the boat, at their feet, they were well off shore, and close to number one buoy. It was the red bell buoy which marked the start of the approach to the harbor. They had been chasing distant gatherings of terns from place to place for quite some time, gassing the motor successfully once. hooking occasional fish. It was then that the motor had quit. There was no sputtering. no slow dying, it just stopped running.

The sudden silence was startling. Without the drone of the outboard he could hear the screaming birds and he could hear them splash as they hit the water. The waves were slapping against the side of the boat, and he could even hear the bailing can knocking about under the stern seat. And over all these sounds was the loud banging of the bell buoy. It was not a ringing like a church bell but a flat metallic slamming of the four hanging clappers against the heavy metal of the bell within them. There was a rhythmic cadence to the waves but the clanging of the bell seemed strangely out of synch. Chained to the seabed by its concrete anchor, seventy feet down, it seemed to protest in a non-melodious and uneven beating with two or three quick beats and then nothing on the next wave, like an arrhythmic heartbeat.

His father had first checked to see if they needed to add gas, and then had repeatedly tried to restart the motor. He had put his foot across the boat and braced against the far gunwale, then leaned forward , grasped the starter- cord handle and pulled it angrily. Ten pulls, twenty pulls and no results. He tipped up the motor, got out the tools and removed the spark plug. He cleaned the contacts and dried them and tipped the motor back into the water. Ten more pulls and still not a cough or sputter. Billy had looked back at his father then, and had seen it: The sudden grimace...the loss of color in his face...the slumping forward holding his chest.

"Dad, are you okay?"

"Yeah, just tired. Why don't you pull this a few times while I catch my breath?" But he wasn't okay and they both knew it. Billy had helped his father to move forward to the bow seat and had gone back to try to start the motor. Looking over the stern he could see that they were a long way out. Sandy Neck was a low outline against the gray sky. The wind had freshened a little and was now out of the north, which would be in their favor. Also, the tide had turned. The current was carrying them slowly in the direction of the harbor mouth. The motor refused to start.

"Hang on, Dad. We have a little rowing to do. We'll get back in and take you to the Cape Hospital to be checked out. "

"I'm fine, just a little bushed. I don't need a doctor. But, yes, I guess it's time to start rowing. I'll give you a hand in just a bit. As soon as I rest a little. The damned motor isn't going to start."

So now he pulled wearily on the oars. His father was still slumped in the forward seat, wrapped in every available piece of clothing, but still guiding their progress. "God...damn... God...damn." His back ached so badly that he felt as though he could not move for the next stroke, but he kept up the steady cadence. "Like the waves" he thought; "Like the tide... Raise the oars, feather the blades, lean forward, dip the oars, pull backward. Repeat forever."

Finally they reached the coarse gravel beach at the foot of Scudder Lane. He stepped out over the side of the boat into knee-deep water and pulled the boat up as far as he could on the beach, then he helped his father out of the skiff and walked him up above the high tide line to where he could rest against the side of an overturned boat. He carried the motor to the car, and then the rods and equipment, and finally the fish.

Going back to his father he said, "All right Dad. Let's get you up to the car and get you checked out with the doctors."

"No, I'm good. I just want to head for home."

"Dad, we are going to the Emergency entrance and have them look you over. " His father looked up startled, then resigned, smiled wanly, reached into his pants pocket and pulled out the car keys.

"You had better drive Bill."

THE BRASS BED

I was sipping from my snifter of cognac and watching the flickering flames curl around the front of the split cedar log, eating away at the shaggy bark, when the lights suddenly went out. With no electricity the fire was the only source of either heat or light in the large log cabin. In the other deep leather chair, on the far side of the fireplace, sat my host. Until then he too had seemed to be hypnotized by the flames. Outside it was starting to snow again, and the wind was prying at the edges of the windows, trying to find its way into the dimly lit cabin. Some hours before the anemic winter sun had been devoured by the hurrying snow clouds, and then the night had dropped like a heavy and soft comforter over the cabin. Edwin was not happy. All his money would not help to turn the power back on. Edwin did not like things he could not control.

He slumped in the massive chair, and his eyes darted about the room, as though he feared something. But it was not fear, it was agitation. I had seen Edwin in this mood many times, going back to our sophomore year in college, when we had been roommates. Even then he had been Edwin, not Ed or Eddie. And even then I had been his only real friend. He was well known and highly respected, but he was not liked. I think it was because Edwin was too good at everything he did. Edwin knew that others envied him and that they would like to outdo him. That made them competitors, and they could therefore not truly be friends. Probably that is why he and I were friends. I was not competition because I did not want to compete with him. While I had studied Literature he had majored in Business. When I was at the library he was at football practice. Later when I went on to graduate school he went on to Wall Street. By the time I had a PHD in American Literature he had his tenth million. Along the way we had each made one marriage, and he had followed his with a divorce, whereas I was still married and now had two married children.

I studied him by the firelight. His heavy shoulders, his strong neck, his massive physique still told you he had been a football player. He still had all his hair, and it did not show much more than a trace of grey at the temples. Hard exercise, jogging and handball had helped him to keep in shape, even thirty years later. Edwin was disciplined, as I had never been. He had routines which he obeyed. He kept the finest food and liquors for his guests but was moderate in his own diet and drinking. But the agitated shuffling of his feet on the deep carpet and his repeated glances at the lightless lamp indicated his mood.

"Some damned fool hick with one too many beers under his belt probably ran into a light pole up on the highway!" He said.

"So, lets relax, then. The steaks were good and the cognac is great! I'm glad the lights waited until we were through eating before they decided to quit."

"It could be hours before they get them back on. Damned inefficiency! I tell you, in New York they'd have them back on in minutes."

"Well, we aren't in New York. I guess in the San Juan Mountains of Colorado it isn't as important." This was just one of Edwin's four homes, the other three being an apartment in Manhattan, an estate in Westchester County and a villa on the Costa Brava. We had flow out just that day from the New York suburb in Edwin's Learjet. As with everything else that Edwin did, he was an excellent pilot, and as prepared as he always was, there had been his jeep SUV parked at the airport outside of Durango.

" I would really like to knows how Tokyo is opening. The way stocks closed in our markets today I'm a bit concerned. I'm long the Yen and the Dollar was acting weak at the bell yesterday."

"I wish I could help, but we don't even have phones. If you had a plain phone instead of this high-tech equipment that needs power maybe we could get out." In the room off the living room where we sat Edwin had installed a number of computers, copiers, printers, telephones and other electronic equipment all reliant upon satellite communications. It was identical to the equipment in each of his other homes. But now it was dead, and here in the narrow valley even the cellphone didn't work. We could have taken the jeep into town, in spite of the snow, or even just far enough to get cellphone coverage, but that would have been too primitive to suit Edwin. So we sat in the light of the flickering fire.

"Edwin, this is as good a cognac as I have ever had, Courvoisier Napoleon isn't it? We have had a marvelous meal. This time of year there will be nobody coming down here by the river. We ought to enjoy the absolute quiet and solitude. It sure as hell beats Manhattan in my book."

"Oh I know, you were always the laid back one. You know how to relax: I don't know how you do it. The currency markets can get along without me, I realize that, but I have trouble letting go, even when I'm here. And the power outage is more of an irritation than a crisis. I envy you in a way.

"Edwin, what you need is a brass bed."

"What?"

" A brass bed. Didn't I ever tell you about the brass bed? "

"No, I don't think so."

"Here, pour me a little more of that magnificent brandy and try to relax. There isn't anything we can do about the power outage anyway, so sit back, uncork that bottle and I will tell you my story of the brass bed.

"It must have been at least twenty years ago, because the kids were still small. Sara and I had taken them to Mexico during Spring Break. Molly was probably about twelve and so that would have made Davey eight. I remember that we said we were lucky their school vacations coincided with my break at the University. So we went to a remote seaside village on the Sea of Cortez, figuring it was small enough and far enough off the beaten path to let us get away from the other tourists. We didn't realize that every rich Mexican in the entire country had taken his family to the seashore. It was a madhouse! We had made a reservation at a rundown motel at the end of the beach so we had a place to stay, but everywhere we went there were crowds.

"On the third day Sara and I decided we would try to get away and find some of the quiet we had come for. I remember I was driving an old Dodge pickup with a camper shell. Luckily it was four wheel drive. Just beyond the motel, where the pavement ended, a sandy track took off up the coast, paralleling the shoreline, but in away from the water, cutting through the Sonoran desert. I had been told that it went on for about thirty miles, ending at a Seri Indian village. The Mexican lady who managed the motel warned me that she had been told the road was passable with a truck, but difficult. In addition, I had heard stories about the Seri Indians at the end of that thirty miles. According to local tales they had been, until quite recently, cannibalistic, and had lived on Tiburon Island, visible across about five miles of water from our motel. A few years before, though, the government had moved then to the mainland where they could keep a closer eye on them. Evidently fishermen had disappeared from time to time and it was thought that maybe the Seris had not entirely given up their customs. There was no evidence that the fishermen had ended up as Seri stew but the locals liked to scare the tourist by telling them so.

"I was more apprehensive about the less bizarre stories that I had heard that the Seris at the village were very surly and uncommunicative. They tolerated the occasional adventurer who made the long trek, in order to sell them baskets and woodcarvings, but were not at all friendly. It was also said they would steal from you or your vehicle if you did not watch them. However, Sara seemed less concerned than I, and the kids, of course, thought it would be a great adventure to see real cannibals. So we started off.

"As it turned out we never got to the Seri village anyway. About five miles along we came to a fork in the road, if you could call it a road. It was just a pair of sandy ruts across the desert. In places the onshore wind had filled the ruts with soft powder that sank under our tires. We were in constant fear of bogging down and wondering what we would do to get help if that were to happen. The more traveled road went to the right, the Seri village, but the road to the left looked a bit firmer. In addition, it was obviously a route to the shore. It seemed a good excuse for not continuing the long miles of bad driving to a destination that worried me. So, checking with Sara, and after listening to the complaints of the kids, I turned to the left, along the less traveled pair of sandy ruts. I hoped we could find a quiet cove or beach where we could sun bathe and swim; where the kids could play and perhaps I would be able to do a little fishing from the shore.

"The road was terrible! It too had had long stretches of deep sand in which I could do nothing except hold the accelerator to the floor and careen madly ahead, so as not to bog down. There were bumps that threw us about, but I didn't dare go slowly even in four-wheel drive. In addition the Saguaro cactus and the Palo Verde were so close to the sides of the big truck that we were constantly brushing by them, and one heavy branch yanked the left outside mirror clean off, to where it was dangling by wires, but I didn't dare stop. I would have turned around if able but there were no wide spots or pull offs, so we careened ahead. It was hilly country sloping down to the west, toward the Gulf. Occasionally we would top a rise in the road and be able to see the sparkling blue water. I felt sure we would be able to turn around when we got to firmer surface near the water. So we slued and bounced ahead going faster than I really wanted to but having no choice.

"Suddenly we were there. As we came around a dune I had to lean on the brakes and slide in the soft sand to keep from going right into the drink. There was a line of grass and rocks, a small strip of beach and then the water. Edwin, it was one of the most exquisite places I have ever seen. We were facing a cove about a quarter of a mile wide. The narrow white sand beach in front of us curved gently to meet rocky peninsulas at both our left and right. Those craggy points jutted outward and then curved around to protect and partially enclose the resultant cove. The heights of both peninsulas were circled, very high, by immense flocks of frigate birds and I could see many more roosted on the high outcrops. Below the cliffs there were pelicans, skimming just inches over the crests of the waves, and occasionally plummeting awkwardly into the water, to emerge with a fish in their bills. Looking out to the open Gulf beyond, there were even some dolphins, rolling half out of the edge of a line of breakers. Closer in the water was light green, and so clear it was difficult to know where air ended and water began. It was shallow and sandy in front of us and shelved out gradually into deep water. There were no people on the beach and no vehicles to be seen. Were it not for the tire ruts we had followed in one could almost believe that no one had ever been there before. There was a pristine beauty that defies description. Even the kids seemed a little awestruck. It was like the feeling one gets on entering a cathedral. The immensity of the place and its imposing beauty bring about an involuntary silence. I felt the same way when I looked at this remote cove. Edwin, you should have seen the place."

"So what did you do? Could you turn

around?

"Well, we saw that the road did not end there, but made a sharp right and went around behind a dune, toward the north end of the cove. I still wasn't sure about turning around and we had all immediately decided to spend the day there, so I continued to follow the sandy track. As we went around the dune and up a slight rise imagine my surprise. There in front of me, on the sand just back from the beach, was an old fashioned brass bed!"

"Ah, yes, the fabled brass bed. I was wondering when you would get to that."

"It was just there, near the beach, with a mattress and all. Under it we could see a couple of cardboard boxes that looked as though they were filled with clothes. To the right, perhaps fifteen feet from the bed, was a circle of stones; a fireplace, with two blackened aluminum pots on the sand beside it. Two wooden posts had been set into the sand. One was near the bed and the other beside the fire pit. Stretched between their tops was a wire, and hanging on that wire, drying in the desert sun, were a number of fish.

'Tom, who do you suppose would be camping out here in such a lonely place? Sara asked.

'Well,' I answered 'I don't' think its Americans. It looks too permanent. But I don't think its Seris either. They probably wouldn't have the bed.'

'Look Tom, there's someone coming up the beach. It looks like an old man. Maybe we aren't supposed to be here. Should we just leave?'

'No. Let's talk to him. All he can do is tell us to leave. Besides, I want to know about the brass bed' I answered. As he approached I could see that he was, indeed, a Mexican. He was small and thin with a wispy grey beard. His trousers, which had probably once been white, were frayed at the bottom, above his bare feet. They were held up by a length of rope as a belt. His shirt was a faded blue and was torn at the shoulder and under the left arm. He held an empty Tecate beer can with heavy monofilament fishing line wrapped around it in his left hand. As he walked up toward the window of the truck he was gesturing as though to say we should leave. I rolled down the glass, feeling the dry desert heat overcome the air conditioning. It was a lined face with crow's feet at the corners of the eyes and deep creases in the cheeks which disappeared under the scraggly beard. His hair had not been cut in a long time and looked as though it rarely experienced a comb. This was the face of a man who lived outdoors. The eyes had a squint that told of days on the ocean, and his skin was the dark brown that is only developed after many years in the sun. When I spoke to him in Spanish a smile of relief and delight split his face, revealing a few remaining stubs of teeth.

"I apologized for disturbing him and told him how beautiful we thought the cove to be. That pleased him and he nodded repeatedly. Then I asked him if we could have his permission to swim in his cove and fish from his rocks.

'Ah, *senor*, the cove is not mine nor is the beach and the rocks. Most *Turistas* come here and do not ask me if they can swim or fish. They just do so.' He said in Spanish. 'Please enjoy yourselves. It is, as you say, a beautiful place. It is my home, but I do not own it. It is part of the *Gobierno*.'

'Do you live here, then?'

'*Si Senor*. That is my bed and my fire pit. I live right here and catch fish for my food. Sometimes I do a little work up at the *turista* beach, so that I can buy tobacco and salt and flour. But most of the time I am here.'

'And you sleep in the big brass bed?'

'Yes, that was my father's bed up in Hermosillo. After both my parents died my sister kept the house, but I got the brass bed. That is my inheritance.'

'But what do you do when it rains?' I asked.

'It does not rain this time of year.'

'And in the rainy season?'

'Then I move to a cave which is around the other side of that black hill over there. But it is up high, away from the water, so I have to walk a long way to get to my fishing. Also, I do not like the cave because of them.'

'Because of who?'

'The spirits that live in the mountains, the old ones. They do not like to have me in their cave. I can sense them around me and it makes it difficult to sleep. It is better when it is not the rainy season and I can live here, near the water.'

"I looked at the beer can he held in his hand, with the fishing line wrapped around it. It was, of course, his fishing reel. I had often watched Mexican boys fishing off the rocks in the same way. They would hold the can in one hand and with the other they would swing the lure in a large horizontal circle over their heads, gathering momentum before letting the lure sail out over the water. The line would spiral off the end of the can, using the same method as my expensive spinning reel. Then they would retrieve the line, hand over hand, often flipping a Sierra or Barracuda up onto the rocks where it would be left to shudder its life away, while the fisherman went back to his primitive but effective work. But looking at the old man's rudimentary tackle I saw that the lure dangling from an old wire leader at the end of the monofilament was beaten and scarred. The chrome had been battered away by the teeth of many fish and the edges of many rocks. Had it not been a lure I was very familiar with, a Castmaster, I would have been hard put to identify it in that condition.

'Do you catch many fish with that?' I asked, pointing to the lure.

'*No senor*, it does not catch fish like it used to. I found the lure in the rocks, a long time ago. Some rich *Americano* had lost it. It was a very good lure, and caught many fish. But it is not so good now, so I do not always get enough fish.'

"We spent a good part of the day on that little beach. I can picture it still. I tell you, it was the most beautiful place I had ever seen. Before we left, with the sun dropping down toward the offshore island and the water still translucent, I rummaged through my tackle box in the back of the pickup. I found a spotlessly new Castmaster lure. As we drove back through the old man's campsite, past the marvelous brass bed, I rolled down the truck window. When he came up to me I thanked him for the use of his beach and then leaned out and handed him the lure. His smile topped off a wonderful day.

"After we got home from the trip I continued to think about that old man and his Castmaster lure. When I felt as though I was having a bad day or a bad week I would think about the beach in Mexico and remind myself that I could always get myself a brass bed and a Castmaster lure. I must have voiced that from time to time because the next year, on our anniversary, Sara surprised me with an unusual present...an old-fashioned brass bed that she had found in a garage sale. She said it was to remind us both that the pleasures of life did not have to be complicated. That brass bed is in our guest room. Every once in a while when the snow is three feet deep and I am really stressed by my work I go in and look at it."

The fire had burned down to softly glowing embers and the room was quite dark. It was still snowing outside and my cognac snifter was empty. I looked across to where Edwin was still slumped in the leather chair, deep in thought. I wondered what the impression of my story might have been. "Well?" I asked.

"Very interesting," He murmured. "Just a brass bed on the beach. I wonder what it would cost to run electric lines down to that little cove."

THE MINISTRY

Ah, Tahiti, here it was before him after so many years of anticipation. But not under the best of circumstances, unfortunately. This was supposed to be, Steven reminded himself, a therapeutic trip. He sleepily stumbled down the steps from the 757 plane just after dawn on an April morning. He had arrived on his long over-the-ocean redeye flight, with another flight to follow almost immediately. The next was to be a much smaller local airline flight to a lesser-known outer island. He had wanted to get away completely and even Papeete seemed, as he made his plans just days earlier, too busy and worldly. But an hour flight would take him to an island with just one acceptable place to stay, his agent had told him, a group of about two dozen bungalows along a small white beach, nestled in a grove of coconut palms, with a small swimming pool, a dining terrace and absolute quiet and privacy. That is what he craved at that time. The two young children were with their paternal grandparents for "As long as it takes, Steven", as they put it. He planned to sleep, read, enjoy French wines and French and Polynesian cuisine, and perhaps, if boats and guides were to be found, try to catch a Wahoo, Mahi-Mahi or whatever was available. He had fished in many places for many varieties over many years, but had not read up on what was to be encountered in the waters around this remote island to satisfy his fishing passion, nor what facilities were available for hire.

A short walk through the airy and open terminal took him to Air Tahiti. Shortly he and a few other passengers were led by an attendant across the tarmac toward what appeared to be a disturbingly small and flimsy looking aircraft. But then the group was led right past that plane, and to an even smaller one beyond. This was not what he had anticipated, but now he was committed. The last to board, he sighed and reluctantly climbed into the tight seat next to the pilot, with the other passengers already shoehorned into the seats behind him. As the single engine's volume rose to a deafening roar the plane accelerated, bumped, seemed to hesitate, then finally fluttered into the air, and over the lagoon that looked as though it was just feet below them. But his apprehension quickly melted to delight as they rose over the lagoon. He had been sleeping earlier, on the approach to Faaa

Airport that served Papeete, but now he could see the turquoise water of the lagoon below him, with coral heads jutting up near the surface, almost white in the early morning light, and the palm trees along the shore leaning out over white sand. As they gained altitude they suddenly crossed the outer barrier reef, lined with a band of surf, and then over the deep blue of the Pacific beyond. Here, he thought, was what he had been looking for. It was all new, yet it fulfilled all of the pictures he had imagined over the years as he had read about the fabled islands of French Polynesia. He had, as a boy, read *Mutiny on the Bounty*, and there to his right was Matavai Bay where she had been anchored. Bligh had walked that beach, as had Fletcher Christian. His reading had moved on to the rest of the *Bounty* Trilogy and then everything he could find by Nordoff and Hall. Next were short stories and then books by

Somerset Maugham and then he had gone on to Michener , Stevenson and Melville. It should not, he thought, be this beautiful. Those were books, far removed from his real and prosaic world of the twenty-first century. "Yes this is beautiful, but I will be disappointed," he whispered to himself.

They passed over two other islands, high peaks in the center, covered with green, a fringe of white beach, a clear lagoon, and surrounded by a reef, dotted with small islands that bordered the endless ocean. From this altitude they looked pristine and perfect, just as he had imagined. Then they were there, and dropping onto the runway and taxiing to a thatched roof over wooden benches that served as a terminal. A short taxi ride part way around the island took him to the small resort. I was down a crushed coral road, a half-mile from the paved road that circled the island, and was on the edge of a small bay, alone. His bungalow was the last one to right, down the beach from the reception area and dining terrace. It was lightly built, with a palm thatched roof. Inside he had just a bedroom and bath, cooled only by the breeze off the lagoon and by a whirling ceiling fan directly over the big king size bed. There were steps out the door directly to the sand of the beach. As he stood at the door and looked out he again saw the stunning turquoise of the calm lagoon, starting just a few yards from his feet, and noted an underwater coral bar, lighter colored, curving from his right and making an arc out toward deeper water. Perfect for snorkeling, he thought. Beyond he could see the white line of the Pacific Ocean swells crashing unendingly on the outer reef, but the distant sound reached him just loudly enough to be soothing without being obtrusive. Well, so far so good, he thought.

Reading and a nap under the cooling fan were rejuvenating and led him to dig his mask, snorkel and fins out of his luggage and walk out for a swim before lunch. The array of fish, yellow, purple, green, red, banded and spotted and glowing, some as transparent as glass and others black as ebony, in uncountable schools, flashed by him on all sides. The water went from two feet to about ten feet deep as he moved toward the end of the small reef. The water was just cool enough to be refreshing without being cold. He was, he decided, really in the paradise of his dreams. All that was lacking was the people of his imagination. He had yet to see the beautiful and accommodating women who had been painted by Gauguin and written about by Michener. Oh yes there had been the girl at the reception desk, in her *pareau*, with a small flower behind her ear, but she seemed a bit heavier and less alluring than his imagination had portrayed. Yes, and the man cleaning the pool was muscular, brown, smiling, cheerful and appeared to be carefree. The huge boisterously laughing woman who had shown him his room was every bit the image of "Bloody Mary" in South Pacific. The size of the colorful cloth rectangle called a *pareau* that was elaborately tied over her immense girth had to have been an extra-extra-large. Even the pilot of the small plane was whistling a tune as he landed on the grass runway, and the taxi driver, introducing himself as Hiro was dressed in nothing but shorts and a loose fitting shirt, barefoot, and talked pleasantly in pigeon English about the charms of his island. So far so good, but he knew the romance would be missing

The other guests at the terrace for lunch were mainly speaking French, which he could not understand.

Communicating with the waitress was largely sign language. However the menu prices were in French Pacific Francs which he knew were worth around a penny apiece so that was easy. And the great thing was that what you saw was what you paid. Tipping was not acceptable and there was no tax. And the tropical salad he randomly chose without knowing what the menu said was excellent. Half of a small and sweet local pineapple had been hollowed out, the pineapple had been diced, mixed with a sweet and delicious dressing, combined with small shrimp and put back in the pineapple. Even the local beer was very good. Still no problems. He looked around the terrace, at the dozen or so tables, many, like his, up close to the low railing toward the water. They were all evidently tourists, however a number of the women had taken to the local attire, with flowered and colorful *pareaus* tied in the manner they had, he would learn later, been recently taught. The loose flowing fabric, covering yet revealing, made even the least attractive look somewhat more enticing. Just one table down, the threesome, caught his attention. A very tall man, a small woman and a boy. The man could not have looked more like an American tourist, with his light complexion, his very tall stature, his athletic build, and most of all, his clothing. Not to say it was not attractive. It was "resort stylish" with light green shorts, a brightly flowered shirt, spotlessly clean low white sneakers over white socks, and a floppy hat with a wide brim to protect his very non-tropical skin from the tropical sun. "I bet she picked out his outfit." He thought. The boy was perhaps ten and looked like a small copy of his father. "She had apparently dressed him too." he thought. But then his attention turned to the woman. She was different. Brown skinned, black flowing hair, an oval face, sparkling eyes that kept darting toward the view of the lagoon,, but then coming back to smile possessively at the boy. In a *pareau*, bright red, she looked like the vision of the Tahitian maidens he had anticipated. She was truly lovely. Next to her tall companion she looked extremely small, and was slimmer than the Gauguin models of the paintings. The *pareau* give just the hint of a small waist, and suggested no bra. Here was the image of the girls that swam out to the Bounty and frolicked uninhibited with the British sailors. He could not keep from glancing back again and again. He felt a stirring he had not had since before the night Janet had died, and he pushed it aside in his mind. It came, therefore, as a big surprise when he overheard this supposed Polynesian Princess calling the boy Son, and speaking to him in a very clear and unaccented English. "Ah, there goes the illusion."

Further down the terrace was a couple who could only have been French, although he could not hear their speech. Tall and gaunt, with a large and sharp nose, the man was a modern image of DeGaul, Steven thought. And beside him the wife was equally thin, looking aristocratic and acting, he could tell, demanding in dealing with a waitress who was uncharacteristically not happy. "I bet they are Parisians on vacation." whispered Steven. Back from the railing were a table of six. Three younger couples, evidently traveling together. Near them were seated a bearded older man, two men with their wives, or so it seemed, and four teenagers. "I guess Grampa has taken the sons and their wives or daughters and their husbands, along with their kids, for a free vacation.

He seems to be in charge."

It was then that a very different couple walked up to the terrace and waited for a table. As they stood he studied them with interest. They were perhaps in their thirties, although the man might have been older. What was immediately noticeable was that he was not dressed for the tropics. He had on long trousers, black, and a white shirt, open at the collar, but suggesting it usually had a necktie inserted. In a world of sandals or sneakers or even barefoot, he wore heavy black shoes and socks that just gave the feeling of oppressive warmth in this hot and humid climate. Somewhat shorter than the lady, he was also overweight enough to make it seem as though he must be sweating profusely under all those clothes. He wore rimless glasses over a clean shaved face. His appearance was unsmiling without actually frowning; perhaps stern would be the term for his look. But the lady was all smiles. She spoke in French to the hostess that seated them, as evidently requested, at a table across the terrace from where he sat, so that they were away from the water, and in a small alcove of bougainvillea, the purple flowers framing them. It put them in a more private location, hardly visible by anyone else. The wife, as he assumed she must be, was wearing a bikini, covered modestly with a shawl and had silvery sandals on her small feet. Nevertheless, the shawl could not disguise her buxom and shapely body. Red hair dropped well below her shoulders and she had to push it from across her face whenever she nodded, as she did often as she listened intently to her companion.. Even from across the terrace it was difficult for him not to take notice of her ample cleavage when she leaned forward, yet her husband seemed preoccupied and unconcerned. For the second time in just a few minutes, Steven realized that he was thinking thoughts that he had avoided for the last three months. He again attempted to put them aside, but found it difficult to not stare. Twice he looked away quickly when she suddenly glanced in his direction, perhaps being aware of his focus, but she did not change her position or actions. Steven ordered another beer and tried to change his focus to the beach and the coconut palms in the white sand. When he looked back their lunch had arrived and she was turning back to the table and her husband. The two of them joined hands, bent their heads and the man said a few words of benediction before they started to eat. Steven left the rest of his beer and went back to his bungalow.

The next morning he went to the reception area and asked them to call a taxi for him. The same car as the day before screeched to a stop and the same driver, Hiro, greeted him as an old friend. Perhaps he was the only taxi on the island.

"You want tour of island for day? Cheap. We see whole circle. Go to *Marae* that is like where ancestors did dancing for gods. See missionary churches. See waterfalls and blowhole?"

"Not today, Hiro. Maybe another day. Do you know where I can set up a fishing trip? "

"Oh yes monsieur. I have friend with fishing boat at town dock. Good boat. He know how to catch big fish. Mahi-mahi, shark, wahoo, big marlin. He get them good. I take you there? He my friend, give you big cheap."

Yes, let's go."

The boat was old, but tidy and the fishing equipment looked quite new. The skipper, Tamatoa, was a greying native dressed in a pair of threadbare shorts, a faded tee shirt imprinted with a Boston

Red Sox logo, and he was barefoot. Through the help of Hiro a deal was soon made. The price was reasonable so he set up a date for the next morning for a trip, outside beyond the reef. Hiro would, of course be picking him up at the resort and taking him back to the town landing early the next morning. He told Tamatoa he wanted to catch, if possible, a wahoo, which was still on his bucket list, or if not perhaps some Mahi-Mahi which was on his list of delicacies.

"I take you now to shop that sells black pearls? " asked Hiro. "You buy pretty necklace for your pretty lady in America. That okay?"

"No Hiro. There is no pretty lady in America anymore. Not long ago you could have made a sale but now I just want to go back to my bungalow, here in Tahiti, not America; at least not yet."

That afternoon, after nap, he decided to again swim along his private reef with his snorkeling gear. The day was sunny, hot and humid and even in the bungalow with the fan on high he was too warm. A languid drift in the cool water would soothe but invigorate him, and it was still a long time before dinner. He worked his way out again and at exactly the same spot as the day before a fish, apparently the same fish, about a foot long, so pale and blue it was as though he was looking through it, approached him. "I bet," he thought, "That she will try to drive me away again." Just then the fish charged directly at his face mask and only turned away at the last instant. Then it swam in a tight circle and repeated the show. "I'm truly sorry, Madame Fish, to be invading your territory. You certainly are beautiful but you don't scare me. Can't we just share the place for a little while? Are you guarding your children? That is good, and I should not be interfering, but I am not going to stay long. That's what I should be doing too, guarding my nest, not swimming in a lagoon on some remote tropic island. You are right, Madame Fish, Keep your distance and scare away danger. As you know, there are always sharks around. But I am not a shark, trust me." He swan further, to the end of the reef, and saw in the deeper water further out, a dark shadow sweep by. "Go hide with your children, Madame Fish."

After nearly an hour of paddling among the thousands of tropical reef fish he turned and headed back to shore. With his head submerged, breathing through the snorkel, he had not looked back to land until now, which he did to ascertain his direction. There was someone on the beach in front of his bungalow. He could make out a person; it looked like a woman, lying on a beach towel in the shade of a palm tree. In the dappled light it was hard to make out more. But then as he got closer he saw that it was, in fact a woman, and the first thing that struck him was that she was topless. Getting closer he saw flaming red hair over her shoulders and knew immediately that it was the woman of the stern husband, the prayer before lunch and the beautiful body that had been framed in the alcove of bougainvillea at lunch the previous day. All this ran through his mind, but most of all he felt embarrassed to walk up on her. She looked up at that same time, saw him, and instead of hiding herself she waved gaily at him to come ashore. As he got closer, but not too soon for him to miss the spectacular display, she picked up her towel and wrapped it modestly around her body.

"Topless is normal in these islands, you know." Sorry if I shocked you. I didn't think anyone was around and I felt daring. I wanted to see what it was like to be as uninhibited as these people seem to be. I remember you at the terrace yesterday. You were alone. Is this your place?"

"For the next few days anyway. Yes just me. Taking a break from the fast life in The States. But I really didn't expect a mermaid on my doorstep. It wasn't in the brochure. However, I'm not complaining. You were with your Husband? Vacation?

"Correct on both. But we are in a bungalow over on the garden side. They are cheaper than what you have and that was the best the congregation could spring for. So I came over to use the beach, and it looked like nobody was home at your place so I camped out here. Sorry to intrude. I will get out of your way."

"No, please don't rush. It's nice to have someone to talk to. Traveling alone is new to me. Especially since it's the first conversation I ever had with a mermaid. But what happened to your tail? You grew feet. '

"We desert mermaids all have feet. There is not much water in the Rio Grande."

"Albuquerque?"

"Nearby. Oh, by the way, my name is Miriam."

"I'm Steven, Steven Phelps. Here from San Francisco."

As you may have guessed watching us at lunch my husband is a minister in a church. A very generous church. Every year they take up a collection and send us on a paid trip. This year it was Tahiti. That was my choice, and actually it cost more than the collection plate yielded. But I wanted a complete escape. All year I am the dutiful preacher's wife. Bake sales, teach in the Sunday School, hold ice cream socials, visit parishioners that are sick. The whole nine yards. Not that I am complaining. My life is helping people, and I am good at it. Sometimes, though, it is nice to get out of the spotlight, if you know what I mean. Earnest would be happy anywhere. I got him into a bathing suit and out on by the swimming pool yesterday afternoon, but he refused to put on sunscreen and now he has a raging sunburn. So he is in the room, probably reading his bible or working on his book."

"Sounds dull! You should be seeing more of the place." In his mind suddenly he recalled the books about the early missionaries on these islands; the dour New England Puritans with their subservient wives, forcing the natives into Mother Hubbards to cover their 'wicked nakedness'. "How does he feel about you sunbathing topless?" he said with a laugh. It doesn't seem very 'ministerial'.

"Oh, no problem.. I do my thing and he does his. In his way he is having a marvelous time too. And we really like to be here together . We do tours, see sights, go to dinner, talk and compare our observations. I am afraid I have given you the wrong impression. This isn't the 1800's and the missionaries I am sure you have read about. Our love, our marriage and our ministry are all one. We just unwind in different ways. If for me it's lounging in my bikini that is fine with him. If reading scriptures in paradise but not seeing the paradise suits him, that's okay with me." She stopped, looked down at the sand for a time, then turned back to him. "Sorry. I didn't mean to react that way. To be honest, I knew you were out there snorkeling. I could see you, and knew you were the man at the terrace yesterday. I didn't come here to embarrass you though. I really did want to get some beach time, alone mostly, and we are back away from the beach so I thought I would look for a quiet corner, and yours fit the bill. But I didn't mind when I saw you out there. Yesterday you looked so sad at lunch. I saw you looking me over, but it didn't feel lecherous, it was wistful I thought. I kind of liked the attention and played a bit to it, of course. But really I wondered why you were alone, in such an idyllic place and was not happy. Like I said, my business is people, and you interested me.

"No problem. I didn't think it was so obvious. Yes, I guess it is sadness too, but really I am just trying to escape for a while. Long story."

"And you don't want to talk about it? We all want to escape once in a while but we don't run off alone to the most remote island we can find." She laughed. "In fact, most of us can't afford to or perhaps we would. That's okay, I ask too many questions. People and their problems interest me. I guess that is a requirement in my job."

"No, I can afford it fine. I do Mergers and Acquisitions in my financial firm in San Francisco. Actually I live in Sausalito, across the bay. My two kids are there now, with their grandparents while I go play in the islands. My wife is gone. So you can see why I am alone and a bit sad. But I will get over it. Just meeting you has been good. Maybe at another time I will feel like I want to tell you more."

"Sure. If you want to talk I'll be around. But right now I had better get back to Earnest. He wanted to go over some of his writing with me before dinner. He's working on another book. It is really very well done. It deals with the first Christian martyrs."

"Say, I have an idea. I am going out fishing tomorrow. I chartered a boat today, and it can take more than just one passenger. It wouldn't cost you anything. You could get a look at the motus, the little islands out along the reef, and see this island from out at sea. You can fish too, if it interests you. We might even get a chance to talk some more. Could you sneak away?"

"Say, that sounds fascinating. I don't know anything about fishing but the day on the water would be wonderful, and I promise you, I don't get seasick. But I would not be sneaking away as you called it. Earnest will think it is a perfect opportunity for me, and I am sure he wants to get some more work done. You're on."

Wonderful! Hiro, my faithful taxi driver will pick us both up, then, outside the reception area at seven in the morning. Too early for you?"

"Never. See you in the morning." And she was gone.

The sun was dazzling as they headed out toward the barrier reef, with Tamatoa expertly and effortlessly threading his way around and past coral heads. It had been already getting warm and humid as they met and got into the taxi a little earlier, but now the breeze was invigorating. Steven, as always, reveled in the feeling of the start of a day of fishing. But this was different. He looked over at Miriam, as she faced into the wind, peering around the edge of the cabin, with her red hair blowing back from under the baseball cap, wearing a long sleeved but light shirt and jeans. "She doesn't look much like a preacher's wife." He thought. "And she really is lovely...Hey, never mind, forget it,"

Soon they had passed through a break in the reef, and out into the dark blue water of the open ocean. He watched Tamatoa as he sewed a large hook into a baitfish that looked like a very large herring, secured it with a bit of wire through the hook eye and around the snout of the bait, and rigged it on one of the lines. The skipper did this while steering the boat with one bare foot on the wheel. They would troll three lines. And for a time they did so with little response. Miriam and Steven sat in the two chairs, not real fighting chairs, just chairs with a built-in socket for the butt or the rods, facing aft and watching the rods as they twitched with the action of the baits behind the wake of the boat.

" You love to fish." Miriam said it as a statement not a question. "It shows. I can see you relaxing and letting go. I hope I haven't intruded."

"Actually I was thinking what a pleasure it is to have you here. Janet, that was my wife, sometimes went with me, and I miss that. But, yes, I have fished for almost anything available, anywhere I was, since I was a kid. Fresh or salt water, bluegills to tuna. I have fished alone on tiny mountain brooks and I have fished on party boats where dozens of us just lined the rail and dangled baited hooks, shoulder to shoulder. It is all fun. But you are certainly not intruding."

"How about your kids? Two I think you told me yesterday. Do they like to go with you?"

"Yes. They are both boys, eight and eleven, and they both are catching the fishing bug. Do you have children?"

"No. Almost did once, but things went wrong. Like you said yesterday, it's a long story, but the upshot is no kids, now or ever. So I am Aunt this or Mrs. that to all the kids in the church. You are lucky, you know. She was about to go on when the center rod suddenly bowed sharply and the reel clicked rapidly as the line stripped out. "You have fish on. Wahoo. You sit, I give you rod" shouted Tamatoa. Steven sat back grabbed the offered rod and plunged the butt into the socket. He could feel the power of the fish as it streaked away from the boat.   Instinct said he was losing too much line too fast. The fish was stripping it out in a hurry, and without thinking he tightened the drag. "No, let run!" But it was too late, there was a sharp twang as the line parted and the fish was gone. "Okay, we find more. Next time you let run until I say." Then he went back to running the boat and the two of them watched the lines for a long time without speaking.

Finally she broke the silence, "I'm, sorry." She said. "You wanted that fish didn't you."

"My fault. I should have known better. I reacted without thinking. Yes, I did want to catch it because it has been a goal of mine, to catch a wahoo. I'll get over it."

"You are pretty good at self-blame, aren't you? It looked to me as though you were doing okay, but you didn't know exactly what to do. That isn't your fault. You have to put it aside and go on fishing, don't' you? Come on, we are here so you can have fun. Smile, there are other fish in the ocean."

"Yes, you're right, of course. I am an expert at self-blame. Maybe that is my problem That, I guess, is really why I am here. Let's forget it. You   never know when another great catch may come along."

"Did you lose another great catch? Did you tighten the drag too much and she broke away? Is that what is bothering you?"

"No, it isn't that way, actually. No separation or divorce or anything. That might be easier. She died. She died in an automobile accident, and I was driving. That was three months ago tomorrow. It really is a very ordinary story. We were not even partying. We were, if you can believe it, on our way home from a PTA meeting. No drinking, no speeding, no distractions, no cell phone or texting. I had the green light at an intersection I had driven through nearly every day for many years. Maybe I wasn't paying attention, because I didn't notice the fast moving car coming at the intersection from my right, or I would have slowed or stopped. And it wasn't a drunk driver or a reckless teenager driving the other care. It was just an older man who had a coughing attack as he was driving, and didn't see the red light. Prosaic as hell, right? But just as deadly. He T-boned the passenger side of my car, Janet's side. Nobody else was even badly hurt, but she was killed. I just wasn't paying attention."

"Steven, I am so sorry. How horrible for you. But you were no more to blame for that than you were for losing the wahoo a while ago. Only the Lord knows why these things happen, but it isn't a reason to quit fishing or to quit living."

"The Lord? Maybe I can blame him instead. Fate and all that. He works, they say, in mysterious ways. Well, there is no mystery to this, in both cases I screwed up. Now my boys don't have a mother, and I don't have much of a life.. But wait, you haven't heard the rest of my melodramatic story. You asked so I will tell you. Perhaps I need a listener, and you have a way of drawing me out, so I will give you the whole thing.

"Fast forward to last week. As I told you, I work in San Francisco but live in Sausalito, so I usually use the ferry instead of driving over the Golden Gate Bridge. It has always been a time to reflect, rest and plan. So I was going home on Wednesday, and feeling, as I had been for the last three months, very depressed. I guess I should have been taking the pills they had prescribed, but I avoid medicines. It had been a bad day at my company. A merger we had been working on for months, a big one, looked as though it was falling apart, and again, I was thinking that I had blown it somehow. The boys had been difficult, undoubtedly because they didn't really understand how or why their mother was gone. It was cold, drizzling and dark out on the bay. Somewhere past Alcatraz Island I went outside and stood at the rail, with nobody around, and looked at the water rushing by. I got to thinking it was offering me an opportunity to just quit. It came and went quickly, but I was really tempted to just climb over the rail and drop into that inviting water.

"The next morning I drove, as usual, to the ferry landing, and was about to go aboard and suddenly found I couldn't. I just didn't dare. It might be too much a temptation next time. I turned around, went home, called a friend in the travel business and booked this trip. I knew I had two kids that depended on me. I knew I had a company to run. I knew I had friends that loved me. I couldn't take the risk. So I booked an open ended escape. I would go back when I was ready. I envisioned silent meditation and sorting out my thinking until I felt I would be able to go back and get on that ferry without fearing I might jump. I thought I wanted to be alone. Then you appeared on my beach, just yesterday, like a mirage, or should I say like a mermaid. So that's it. My family knew, vaguely, why I was coming here, but you are the only one I have been able to tell about that night on the ferry. Thank You."

When he looked at her she was looking down at the deck. At first he thought she was just thinking but then he was surprised to see she had tears on her cheeks. She brushed her face unashamed, and looked up at him. "No, thank you for trusting me with your secret. And, it will be just yours and mine. You know, I don't believe the accident was in any way your fault, and you shouldn't either. In your business it pays to be productive and your thinking now is counter-productive. Right? Also you have two kids that need you now more than they did when Janet was alive. If the merger falls through isn't there another possible candidate in the wings? It seems to me you have an awful lot to live for and nothing too die for." Then they both sat quietly for just an instant, when, suddenly, the starboard reel sang out. "Fish on!" she screamed. Get to work Steven."

It was different this time. He grimly held the rod tip up as the line disappeared. But just when he thought it would never end the fish stopped running. "Now," said Tamatoa. "You hit him good with hook and tight the drag just some, not too much. It is big

Ono, what you call Wahoo. No lose this time." He worked for what seemed a very long time, pumping the fish closer, only to give the line back over and over again. His arms were aching, his back was tired, he had skinned the knuckles of his right hand, reeling furiously. But she was watching intently and he was trying to do everything right. He kept trying to see where the fish was, but the line seemed to be extending to the horizon. Then, unasked, she moved behind him and massaged his aching shoulders as he worked the up and down rhythm to gain line. Her touch was soothing and he almost didn't want the battle to end. But finally the long sleek fish, perhaps six feet long and around a hundred pounds, he estimated, was gaffed and lifted into the boat. Tamatoa exclaimed "You do good. Big fish. Good eat. Take some hotel and they fix for you and lady's eat tonight."

"You did it Steven! See. Yes, I would

like to take a filet back to the hotel, but I will be eating, as usual, with Earnest of course."

When they got to the dock, Hiro was waiting to take them back. Then they walked together down to the bungalows and as he turned to the beach she turned toward the garden area, but stopped. "Steven, thank you. That did me a lot of good, and I think it did you too." Then, to his surprise she reached over, pulled him near her and kissed him fully on the lips. His reaction was instantaneous and he pulled her tight, but she pushed him away laughingly. "Hey, easy. I think you are on your way to recovery. I have to go see if Earnest need anything but it is still early and I may want to go for a swim from your beach a little later if you don't mind."

"Mind? I look forward to visit from a mermaid. Do you have a mask and snorkel?

"Yes."

"Bring them. I have someone I want you to meet."

When she walked up in her bikini a short time later he was in his swimming trunks and waiting, sitting on a towel, under a palm tree, close to the water. Her red hair was brushed back. "You will get that beautiful hair wet if we go in the water."

"Who cares? I'm on vacation. Let's go." She reached down, took his hand and pulled him to his feet. He felt as though he was standing very close to her, and was tempted to reach out and pull her to him again, but she smiled, moved away, and still holding his hand they waded into the warm lagoon, until they got to deeper water and put on their face masks and snorkels. They drifted quietly over the white sand with the coral to their right. Schools of reef fish flashed toward them and parted like a river, only to rejoin beyond them. He suddenly grabbed her hand, and pulled her back, pointing at the threatening open mouth of a Moray eel in a cavity in the reef ahead of them. Then they came to the place he was looking for, a separate column of coral, surrounded by white sand. He beckoned to her and again pointed. There, as he had expected, was the translucent blue fish from the prior two days. Again she darted at them, turning away at the last instant. He looked over and saw, inside her facemask, that Miriam was smiling delightedly. Soon he pointed his thumb back over his shoulder and they turned back toward the beach. As they waded toward shore, their facemasks off, he explained. "You just met Madame Fish. Isn't she beautiful? We are old friends. However, every time I get too close she tries to chase me away. I love her, and her dedication. But I worry about her as she guards her domain. There are too many predators out there, threatening her and her family."

"Sounds familiar." Miriam said as they walked up the little beach to his door. Do you have a towel I can use? I forgot to bring one.

"Sure, come on in." He went back to the bathroom and when he returned she was standing, looking out the door, with her back to him. He walked up behind her and slowly started to towel her red hair as it cascaded down her back. She leaned back against him and sighed, her eyes closed. He turned her toward him and kissed her again. This time she didn't push him away. He could feel the tenseness go out of her as she pushed herself up against him. She reached behind her back and undid the hooks on her bikini top. "The mermaid is back." she said.

"I hope there is more than a scaly tail"

"You had better check." Are mermaids on your bucket list?

"They are now!" He backed away, still holding her until the back of his thighs we touching the bed. "Are you sure?"

"Stop talking and get those silly looking trunks off." She shoved his shoulders and he fell backward awkwardly onto the bed and followed her instructions. She quickly moved forward and slipped out of the rest of her bikini as she bent over him.

Later they were still lying, silently, as the overhead fan blew somewhat cooler air over their still moist bodies. "We both needed that." she said softly. Then, a while later, she got up and started to get on her bikini and tossed him his trunks. "We will be going back tomorrow."

"Back? You're leaving? Back to what?"

"Back to my church suppers and choir

practice. Back to my parishioners, my ill elderly and my children. Just as you will be going back to your children, your work and all your obligations. It's time. I think it is time now for both of us."

"But where can I reach you? You never really told me where you live, or even your last name for that matter."

"No, I didn't."

"Will you be back next year?

"No not here."

"But I just found you. We found each other."

"No Steven, we found ourselves. You have the strength to get on that ferryboat again and I have the strength to hug all those people in front of the church after Sunday services. Remember what we said yesterday? There are lots of other trophy fish in the sea, and you didn't lose the second wahoo. Maybe it won't be another Janet, and it shouldn't be, but it will happen. You are just too beautiful and wonderful to be alone. Go back Steven, your kids and your company need you. I think you are ready to ride the ferry boat again." She was backing out the door and he saw her with the sunlight reflecting off her drying and rumpled but still beautiful red hair. And then she was gone.

THE BUBBLE NET

It was my first fishing trip to Alaska. I had blindly signed up for a trip to a lodge near a town called Craig which the owners had pointed out to me on a map they had under Plexiglas on the high counter at the Hunting and Fishing show in mid-February. It was, they told me, just a quick plane ride from Ketchikan, out to Prince of Wales Island. The impressive changing color slides projected on the wall behind them showed men, women and even children standing in front of rows of enormous fish, hanging from a rack on the end of a dock, with the bay behind them. There was a picture of the lodge, situated above the bay, with the dock extending out into the blue water below. The sky was cloudless and glistening, the mountains, covered with evergreens and without a sign of mankind, rose on either side from the smooth waters behind the proud displayers of their catch. Evergreen covered islands thrust out of the bay to the West. I did not take notice, although I should have, that in spite of the clear sky and the calm water the anglers were all bundled up in sweat shirts, gloves, waterproof pants and boots. I saw the fishing boats tied up to the end of the dock and should have observed that they were not the open and airy center console fishing boats of the tropics, but enclosed cabins. But I was mesmerized by close up pictures of eagles and of whales. In addition here were pictures of happy people seated around a large table about to eat a delicious looking array of huge dishes of steaming crabs, heaps of potatoes and colorful vegetables. The impression was irresistible. It didn't show rain or cold or wind. It didn't depict rough waters or seasick fishermen. There was no hint of five-foot swells coming in from the open Pacific, tossing a twenty-six foot boat in all directions, further out beyond the islands, where the fish were to be found. No mention was made of the wet cold feeling when the tossed seawater ran under your hood, and down your neck under the slickers that were issued to all guests, leaning over the rail and trying to entice the Salmon or Halibut to bite. They didn't have pictures showing the pounding and slamming to your back if you sat, or to your legs if you stood, as the boat fought its way out to the open water. I didn't see anything about the way the rainwater ran up your sleeves when you were reeling in, with or without a fish. So I signed up, gave them a deposit and set a date for the end of the coming June.

The day I arrived could have been used in their slide show. The trip getting there had been flawless. Earlier in the day I had eaten lunch in the Seattle airport. A sourdough bread loaf hollowed out and filled with clam chowder, was far better than airport food is supposed to be, and took just long enough to occupy me until my next flight. Miraculously the flight from Seattle to Ketchikan was almost on time. The four-seater floatplane that was supposed to take me out to the island was waiting at the dock, just a short walk down from the airport. The Pilot looked like a teenager, but flew like an expert as I, his only passenger, took pictures of the Inland Passage and then the magnificent mountains on both sides of us as we crossed through a deep valley to the far side of the island. On arrival one of the pretty girls from the kitchen was waiting at the airplane dock to take me over to the lodge, about two miles, and I arrived just in time for supper. Perfect!

There were over a dozen of us gathered around the table. I was the newcomer and alone. I noted most of the others had come with a friend or two, but I was welcomed cheerfully if briefly into the group before they went back to their conversations which centered on the day's fishing. Everyone had gotten his or her legal limit of one single King Salmon for the day and they had all also caught a number of halibut.

Looking around the table, over the heaped platters of poached halibut, mashed potatoes, corn on the cob and steaming hot biscuits, I took in the group and tried to figure out who they might be. Across from me, the most noticeable was a lovely dark haired woman, apparently with the somewhat older man to her left. Honeymooners? Had she come in deference to his fishing passion? I thought not. It had been remarked by one of the boat captains, Alex, who stood in the kitchen area with a cup of coffee in his hand that her salmon was the biggest of the day, and she had been delighted to have it mentioned. Her apparent husband was smiling proudly at her. No, probably not honeymooners, but he evidently doted on her. They were sharing a bottle of wine, drinking from paper cups. Next to them, scanning clockwise, was a man in his thirties, blond, smooth shaven sportily dressed and immaculately neat. He was obviously athletic and in great shape, with bulging muscles apparent under his shirtsleeves. He was drinking water. With him was a boy, maybe fourteen, apparently his son, who was cramming his mouth with the food, and looking at no one, swigging a bottle of Gatorade. The four others on that side were, they told me, New York City Firemen. They put together an outing like this each year, always in a new place. They talked about fishing together in Florida, Michigan, Padre Island and the Bahamas over the years, but this was their first Alaska adventure. They each had a bottle of cold beer in front of them

To my left was Mike. He was bearded, sixties, jovial, and talkative. He wore an incongruous combination of black shorts over grey sweat pants and a bright green windbreaker, even though the dining area, a part of the big kitchen, seemed quite warm to me. He also wore a Greek fisherman's hat that seemed appropriate with his sunburned round and cheerful face. Short and stocky, he could have passed for a Greek fisherman. Beyond Mike was his friend, Hank, who, Mike quickly filled me in, was a lifelong friend who had fished and hunted with him in many places over many years. Hank was a bit older than Mike, perhaps my age, and a stark contrast to the athlete across the table. His potbelly bulged over his khaki pants that were held up, barely, by a pair of plaid suspenders. He wore an open windbreaker, larger but otherwise identical to the one Mike wore. Later when I saw Hank walk I would note that it was with difficulty, and that he tired quickly. But now, sitting and enjoying the food, he bantered often with Mike. He had a broad flat face and a small nose, and a scraggly grey growth of whiskers which looked as though he had just quit shaving for this trip. His grey hair was still thick but uncombed. I got the impression he was on vacation and was just going to let everything go, and have a good time.

"Welcome to the zoo." laughed Mike. "Me and Hank are kind of regulars. This is out third year. I don't know why I put up with him. Habit I guess. The old coot is more problem than he is worth but what the hell, I had a double room anyway, and he can play Texas Holdem pretty good."

"Ha!" retorted Hank." He just needs someone he can beat. I 'm the one that puts up with a lot. But if it's free I guess I can even tolerate Mike. After thirty years habits are hard to break."

"So, how come you guys are such good buddies. Work together?" I asked.

"Nope. Hank and I came from the same neighborhood in Seattle. Met in the local bar, and started going fishing hunting and drinking together. I'm retired from owning a construction company that I passed on to my son-in-law and my daughter. Hank is still working as a machinist for Boeing. So this is our one big outing each summer."

The last two, seated beyond Hank, were Lee and Cathy, the husband and wife owners of the lodge whom I had met when they sold me on the trip. I turned to see that the picture window behind me looked out across the bay; just about the view in the slideshow that had been so enticing. It was early evening, but also almost the longest day of the year, so it was still bright outside. I would learn, in fact, that we would have very little night, going to sleep and arising in brilliant daylight. The three fishing boats were tied up to the dock; steel boats with enclosed cabins and with a pair of outboard motors on each. Dozens of bald eagles were perched on the nearby trees, scavenging on the small beach to the left and even the landing on the railings of the ramp. They were all intent upon the action on the dock. The fish from the day's catch were being cleaned and filleted by a young man at a cleaning table on the dock and another was taking the prepared fish up to a small shed where I could see they were being shrink-packaged and put into freezers. These would eventually be taken home by the people who caught them. I turned back to my plate, and a sip of my drink.

"That stuff will kill you, you know." Said Mike, pointing to the still nearly full large glass in my hand that I had prepared and brought up from my room right after arrival. It contained ice, a large amount of Scotch and a very small amount of water. "Me and Hank, here, used to use it a lot up until about a year ago. Never touch it now. It'll kill you." But it was said with a smile and I saw a rueful nod on the part of Hank.

Then the conversation at the table turned to the whales. Evidently there had been a number of Humpback Whales seen very near them as they cruised out to the fishing areas that morning..

"Did you see any of them coming up to the top to feed?" asked the Lee, the lodge owner.

"Oh yeah! They were rolling over on the

surface, flipping up their tails and sometimes rolling on their sides with those big side fins out of the water. Really big. I mean the fins. Of course the whales looked huge, and they were spouting water all over the place. There was a bunch of them, all close together." said one of the Firemen. "What do you think those guys weigh, Lee?"

"They can be up around forty tons, and maybe fifty feet long, or more. A lot bigger than our twenty-six foot fishing boats, that's for sure. They are nothing to mess with." Lee had become very serious all of a sudden.

Mike, still grinning and ignoring Lee's change of mood turned to point at Hank. "We tried to feed old Hank here to them but they kept spitting him out. Even the whales didn't want him." They both laughed. "Did you guys hear about what happened last year?" Tell 'em Cathy.

Cathy, our attractive hostess, much younger than her husband, glanced over to him, questioning what she should do. "I don't want to scare our paying guests."

"No," said Lee, "Go ahead. Maybe it's a good idea for them to know."

"Well, okay, it was just about a year ago, I remember because the Kings were still in and I had been too busy running things to get out fishing much and wanted another shot at a King Salmon. So this one-day we had extra space on one of the boats and I turned everything over to Lee and the crew and went out. There was just me, Alex running the boat, and those two bozos to my right." She smiled at Mike and Hank. "It was a real cloudy and rainy day, but the fishing paid off. The clouds were so low that they cut off the top of Baker Island, so we could just see the cliffs coming down to the water, some seals on the rocks and a few other boats around us as we limited quickly on the Kings. It was pretty smooth though, but cold, but we were done on the salmon so Alex brought us inside to look for halibut. That turned out to be slow, but we worked at that for the rest of the day, until it was time to head for the dock. We were all tired, but those two clowns were as comical as ever, and having a grand time. They had been sipping on their water battles most of the day, and somehow I think there was something besides water in the bottles."

Lee broke in to the narration. "You guys know we have no problem with guests bringing alcohol to dinner, as I see a number of you have tonight. It's not my thing, but okay. But we don't want drinking mixed with fishing. It can be a dangerous combination, to everybody. But go on Cathy."

"Have you guys ever heard of a bubble net?" Only Mike and Hank nodded yes. "Well these Humpbacked Whales have an interesting way of feeding. You know, they don't have a bad life. They spend the winter breeding and playing in Hawaii and then the head for Alaska to fatten up on Alaska's huge supply of food in the summer. They have a way to cooperate and kind of herd the herring together for lunch. It's called a bubble net. When they locate a big concentration of baitfish they go way down hundreds of feet below them, usually three or more whales, and they start to swim in a big circle, blowing bubbles. The rising bubbles are a kind of barrier to the herring and tend to concentrate the food, as the whales rise and tighten the ring. Then, when the herring are really bunched up they come shooting up the middle of the ring, with their huge mouths open. The water is filtered out their gills while the baleen traps the fish. The result is that they come tearing upward and right out of the water. Three or more whales suddenly erupt with no warning. A couple of hundred tons of airborne whale put up a big bunch of waves, believe me.

Can you tell they are coming?" asked the lady across the table.

"Kind of. If you are paying attention you may see the bubble ring on the surface, there may be birds over them looking for food, and at the last minute the panicked baitfish start to jump and boil the water.

"Hey, I would like to see that!" put in the teenager, suddenly excited.

"Maybe not too close though." Said his father. "So did you see it happen?"

" I'll get to that. We were headed in. Alex had poured on the power and the wind was behind us. It was choppy and hazy, not good visibility. In the meantime I guess the water bottle and the tossing boat had gotten to Hank. He was starting to look green around the gills, and after while he decided to get rid of a bit of the booze. He went to the stern, kind of watched over by Mike, and was leaning over the transom, next to the starboard outboard, barfing, Alex and I were warming up inside the cabin with the glass door closed, and didn't notice what they were doing.

Suddenly I saw that there were baitfish jumping out of the water all around the boat and realized that we were inside the edge of a large ring of bubbles rising to the surface. I knew immediately what was happening and started to yell at Alex to get us out of there. But by then he had seen it and was already acting. Just as he made a sudden sharp turn to starboard the whales emerged right beside us, towered over us, and slammed back into the water so close we could look them in the eye. The wave slammed against the boat, as we roared out of the ring.

" 'Stop! Man overboard!' I shouted at Alex as I looked back. We had flipped Hank out on the combination of the turn and the wave. We would have to go back in and rescue him. Alex slowed, turned and was starting to head back toward the whale, and toward Hank. Hank was waving his arms, yelling and trying to stay above water, dressed as he was in lots of heavy clothes and with boots. He was pretty close to the boat, but he certainly had a problem.

"But then, would you believe it, we had not one but two men, in heavy rain gear, splashing their arms in that icy water. Mike had gone after his friend. He had pulled off his boots and rain gear but was still pretty weighted down. Alex zipped up close to them and Mike kind of handed Hank up to us. Then we hauled Mike in. Talk about cold! Those guys couldn't stop shivering. The Cabin heater was cranked up; to the max, and we got them to get out of the wet clothes and wrap up in a coupled of blankets from below while we hightailed it for home By the time we got back to the dock the two nuts were joking about it! And that after coming real close, I think, to having Hank drown while we were trying to get to him. So I guess we have a hero in our midst."

"Well, hell," said Mike. Hank can't swim. Who was I going to play Texas Holdem with?

H's an old coot, but I've gotten kind of used to having him hanging around. But let me tell you something, it kind of solved one of Lee's problems. He never did like us drinking anyway, and especially if we were going out on the boat. I guess he knew we didn't have much water in with the vodka in those water bottles but he didn't want to lose some good customers. The little episode with those whales kind of put the fear of God in us. Or me anyway. I'm not sure there is much that can scare Old Hank. But it came time for our drinks before dinner that evening and we sort of decided to skip it. Somehow it got to where we never did get back to having another drink. We still haven't. That stuff will kill you."

UNHOOKED

First it was cocktail time. Dinner would come later, at a small, inexpensive and strictly Mexican restaurant they knew about, with tables right on the sand, a little distance up the beach from the hotel. They would be the only Americans there. They would sit at the metal tables with the name of a local beer stenciled on the top, in folding chairs, at the far west side, to be as near as possible to the breaking surf and as far as possible from the overly loud but still delightful Mariachi music. They would have the fresh from the ocean shrimp again, sautéed in butter and garlic, *al mojo de ajo* it was called, and eat the oven warm *bolillos*, the rolls with their crisp outer crust and their soft and doughy interiors. They would, of course, have cold beers and would enjoy, but from afar, the Mexican music. They would talk Spanish with the waiter. He, the tall young husband was more fluent in Spanish than the diminutive and attractive wife, but she too would be able to understand, and equally enjoy, the conversation. But the cantina would still be in a little while. First it was time to sip cocktails with other Americans in the courtyard of the hotel. It was a part of their ritual; start the evening as tourists with tourists, then become unobtrusive observers with the locals. It was really the second part of their annual ritual that they most looked forwarded to, but the preliminary set the stage for a more complete enjoyment of the latter.

It was still early at the hotel cocktail area, so they had a wide choice of tables. They opted for a small leather-topped wicker table, near the back wall of the big rectangle that made up the central courtyard of the hotel. Around them were potted palms and flowering plants placed around and between the tables that occupied the northern end of the vast tiled patio, near the bar. On all sides of the roofless patio the rooms, connected by verandas, reached upward for three stories, accessed by a pair of white concrete stairways at the two ends. This hotel was the couple's big splurge each year as they stopped in the resort town on their way back to The States. They had again the same corner room on the third floor, front, with a porch toward the Pacific Ocean and another smaller veranda near the sitting area, giving them a view up the small side street. They had wanted that room again, and by arriving early they had gotten it, even without reservations. It was expensive compared to the prices of the other rooms in the hotel and much more than the other places they usually stopped at in their three day drive back home, but compared to US prices was still something they felt they could do once each year.

They ordered margaritas, and sipped them slowly and watched as the patio started to fill. Two tables filled with older people who seemed very familiar with the place. They greeted the waiter, Benito, courteously, and each couple went to a table which, one got the impression, was their usual table. It was fun to observe the people and guess their backgrounds. The young couple surmised and conversed about the fact that they were probably retired Americans or Canadians who spent their winter in the resort town and came in often. They had not come down from the rooms, but rather had entered from the street, so they probably owned or rented on a longer term basis. Another arriving group of five were young, perhaps college students, and after them were another older couple, the wife pushing a walker and carrying an oxygen tank; probably shorter term tourists staying in a ground floor room.

Before long three men, all in khaki shorts and flowered sport shirts, took the table next to them and quickly pulled together three more chairs, obviously expecting more to come. They lounged back, took off sunglasses and hats, displaying deep tans. The largest, a heavy but muscular man with a white beard and a hairless dome of a head led the group. As soon as they were settled he stood up, waved at the waiter, and loudly hailed him by name. "Benito, *scotch y soda para tres,*" he barked with a very non-Mexican accent.

"Yes, Senor Ed, just as soon as I take care of these other people" he answered in English.

"Mexican time." Said Ed resignedly, so that those at other tables, and obviously Benito, could hear him clearly. *"Mañana."*

The young couple watching them and unavoidably hearing them, both unconsciously and simultaneously pushed their chars away, as though to distance themselves from this American, and not be thought one of their group. But there was no way they could avoid hearing the loud one.

The other two men settled into their wicker chairs and said nothing. The one who had come in second was also a big man but clean-shaven and had a thick mane of white hair, carelessly pushed straight back, without a part. .He slumped back, closed his eyes and ran his hands backward through his hair, giving a deep sigh, smiling slightly. The third was a small man, thin and wiry. He looked tired and troubled. His eyes were fixed on the table and he was not smiling. All were in their late fifties or early sixties, the young couple guessed.

"You still pissed?" The leader said loudly, looking at the small man slumped in his chair. It was apparent he wanted the young couple, and anyone else, to hear and take notice. He leaned over and looked down at the smaller man who did not look up. "Hey, let's have a drink and forget it, I'm buying."

"Hell, you ought to be buying. You got all my money."

"Come on Carl, it was a fair bet. You just didn't like to lose. It was you that set the stakes before we left the dock, right? Didn't he call it, Earl? Each toss in a grand, you said, and the guy with the biggest Marlin today gets it all.

"Yeah it was his call." Replied Earl. "Of course we always have a bet, but this did seem a little big. But we both went along. I don't know why you, Carl, should be so unhappy. I lost as much as you did, but it was one of the best days of fishing I can remember. Hell, it was worth it. We all had the same chance of winning."

The overhearing couple had not meant to eavesdrop, yet the scene had been forced on them. Now, though, they were interested, and straining to pick up the rest of the story, if there was one. "Wow, that's a lot of money!" She said softly to her husband. Why would anyone bet that much on such a thing?"

After a bit of though he said, "It seems to me there are two reasons people usually make bets like that. Either because it is an added excitement or because they believe they can win, and usually the latter are the ones who need to have the money and shouldn't be betting. Who would you put in which category?"

"The way they are acting my guess is Ed and Earl were having fun and could afford the bet. Maybe Carl needed to win."

By then Benito had returned with the drinks, and all three men were drinking thirstily. Finally Ed broke the long silence. "Hey, Carl, cheer up. Good drinks and good company after a day on the water. There's no reason to be down. I admit that was a big fish you had on right toward the end. It probably would have beat mine, but it isn't anybody's fault you lost it. You were doing a great job of working him in before he got unhooked. We were all pulling for you."

"You sure?"

"What do you mean by that?"

"Nothing. Forget it."

Martin came with another round of drinks, and put them on the table.

Earl, who had been taking in the conversation and looking concernedly from one to the other of the men said softly, "Come on, you guys, let's not ruin the night. Here come the girls. Lay off the arguing." Three women approached the table, waving across the patio, and threading their way between the tables. Obviously their wives, the young couple thought, and they had evidently been shopping; they were carrying numerous bags and packages.

An angular, and far from pretty brunette with touches of gray, in a flowered skirt and a halter top, briefly nudged the cheek of Earl with a weary half kiss, dropped her bundles on the tile floor and flopped exhaustedly into the chair nearest her husband. "My god, you can't imagine the territory we covered while you guys were out cruising the Pacific. And talk about dirty! They need to clean up this country. Everything smells. But we did find some real bargains. Say, what does a lady have to do to get a drink around here? Earl, will you see if you can get me a manhattan? They probably don't even know how to make one."

Predictably, the young observers thought, the big and slightly overweight blonde went with the big bearded man, Ed, . Dressed in a similar skirt and halter as the others, and with a similar armful of bags of merchandise, she paid no attention to her husband but took the chair beside him. Pulling off her floppy straw hat, and wiping her brow, she asked, "Well, how was the fishing?"

"Really good." Answered Earl" "Five fish for the day. Two each for Ed and me, and Carl got one and lost another beauty. Ed got the biggest one, but not really that big. But anyway we brought them all back, hung them up and got pictures to prove it when we get home."

Wife number three has already settled in too. She was beside her husband, but pushed her chair over closer to Ed. She was younger and did a lot more for the skirt and halter than the others did, and was a stunning raven-haired lady, which contrasted dramatically to her very pale complexion. "Honey," she said to Carl, who was still slumped in his chair, saying nothing, "You should have seen what I bought. You wouldn't believe the fantastic things they can do with silver and gold jewelry in this country. Real artisans. I just couldn't resist some of the things."

"Did you spend all our money?"

"Not yet Honey, but I'm working at it"

"Yeah."

"Come on guys, we are here to have fun." This from the big blonde. "Ed, see if you can get us another drink and then we can go to dinner. How come you are so quiet anyway, Carl? Only time you have said anything is to complain 'cause we are spending money. The deal was you guys fish and we shop. So we are shopping. Your bride is learning fast from us pros." She laughed.

"No, I'm all right. Hated to lose that beauty, is all. Had her hooked good, and then the skipper made a tight turn and she got off. I think he may have circled around enough to cut the line. It was like he wanted me to lose the fish."

"Yeah, the big one that got away." This from Earl. "I think you just didn't know, being new to Marlin fishing, to keep a tight enough line when the skipper gave you some slack. It was really not your fault. He probably looked at your physique and figured you needed some help... Smile Carl, that was a joke!"

"I'll tell you what I think. I saw the big tips Ed gave the skipper and boat boy. I think that when he and the boat boy were below old moneybags over there told them to cut my fish loose so he could win the bet." Ed jumped to his feet, red faced, but his wife grabbed his sleeve, pulled him down and whispered soothing words into his ear.

"All right, you guys, Cool it. We came to Mexico to have fun." She said to the group. "If you can't take it don't bet."

"Bet? What bet?" Said the pretty one. "Carl you promised me before the wedding that you were not doing any more gambling!"

"Oh, never mind honey. Just a competition between us guys. No problem. I shouldn't have said that about the fishing.. Sorry Ed, just kidding. Here come the drinks, let's drop it."

"Sure, Carl. Let's not upset your lady."

From there the voices became less loud and the couple at the next table went back to their margaritas. .Looking back over a while later they saw that the group was engaged in quiet one-on-one conversations. It was apparent that Carl, was still upset and the big blonde was talking earnestly with him. On the other side of the blonde Ed was in deep but quiet conversation with the pretty one. They all finished their drinks. Ed pulled out a large roll of Mexican bills and paid the bill as they got up to go. The big blonde was setting the pace, charging ahead unsmilingly. The beauty was lagging behind with her arm hooked through Ed elbow. The last thing they heard was Earl saying that they were going to look for a place where they could get a pizza and American beer.

For the young couple, the observers, it was time to go down the beach to the tables on the sand and the cold beer, *bolillos* and garlic shrimp.

PERDIDO

"It is good after a day on the water to sit here and sip an icy beer and listen to the music," he thought. The sun had just set, and the afterglow was bouncing off the tabletops. He should have gone home, but the large tip from the American was something Teresa did not know about. Their charter that day had been three Americans. They had taken them out nineteen miles to the far drop off where the color of the water changed and they had been very lucky. Five out of six hooked fish had been landed; nice large striped marlins, beautiful rainbows of color when they were taken from the water, that changed to a dull black as they died flopping on the deck   He had put plastic coke bottles over the bills so as to not get gored. The Americans had taken the noble fish back to the dock where they had proudly had their picture taken with them. Not trophies, but good fish, all over a hundred and fifty pounds. "*Capitan*, you will not tell Teresa about the tips will you? She thinks we are still down there washing down the boat. She does not know we came in early."

"Tell Teresa? Not me. The *Americanos* are buying with their tips. It was a good day, Lorenzo. You did well. When Serafina told me you were to be my boat boy I wondered if you would be able to do it. But it is going well. I do not like to hire my relatives and especially the husband of my daughter, but you have learned quickly. I do not often admit it, but Serafina is usually right about people. After twenty-eight years I have learned that."

"Yes, over a year now we have been fishing together. It is working well. But I have a lot to learn from you. Not the fishing so much now, but how you handle the customers. I still do not know why the big bald one with the beard today was so happy.

But he really passed out the tips at the end. And even after we brought then in early. I am surprised they did not complain."

"No, I did not decide to bring them in early; it was the bearded one that told me it was time to quit. I think he wanted to make sure nobody got a bigger fish than he did. They had a bet you know. Those *gringos* do not know that I understand English. I am just another dumb Mexican, they think. Their bet was a thousand American dollars each on who got the biggest fish today. I wanted to stay out and make sure they got their money's worth, but he was ready to come in."

The cantina was starting to fill with locals, stopping by for a beer or a meal after the day's work. The musicians were playing and signing *rancheros*. Here they did not have to sing *Cuando Calienta el Sol* or *El Rancho Grande* because there was not a large contingent of tourists from The States requesting them, and thinking they were very knowledgeable in doing so. Here they played the songs of the locals. However there was one couple, Lorenzo noted, who were obviously *Americanos*. They had quietly come in and taken a table down near the waves. The Capitan and his son-in-law watched them come in. The man was very tall and quite thin. He wore sneakers, khaki trousers and a knitted shirt. His companion was small and pretty without being beautiful. She wore a light grey skirt, a peasant style blouse and sandals. The two fishermen could tell they were very happy, not only with the cantina but with each other. They chatted in halting Spanish with the waiter, and smiled as they nodded to the rhythm of the music.

"So *Capitan*, if the little one had gotten the big fish at the end he would have won two thousand dollars? But instead the beard won it. Too bad the little one didn't land that fish. It was the biggest we have had on all month. I saw him cruising on the surface at the same time you did. You came up on him well, and then I saw him turn just as I dropped the bait back and then set the hook. I knew he was big. Funny isn't it. They pay to go fishing and they think they are such great fishermen when they get a big one. But they don't even do it. The two important jobs are hooking the fish and then landing it, and we do both for them. We only hand them the rod and get them into the fighting chair after we have set the hook. Doing the drop back and timing the hooking is the art. After that it's just muscle and a few little simple rules like keeping the rod tip up and a tight line. And then when the fish comes alongside they sit back and watch while we grab the wire, bring it up alongside, and haul it into the boat. And they don't even know that if it were not for you, the *Capitan,* and the way you move the boat they could never get close to hooking a Marlin, and if they did they would never be able to get it to the boat without you making sure the stern is always toward the fish."

"Yes, you are right, of course, Lorenzo." The captain leaned back and half closed his eyes as he looked off toward the sea. "But the money is good and the life is good. I have fished these waters since I was just a boy, Lorenzo. It is a good life, being on the water, and if I am paid to do it is even better. Those Americans don't know it, but they are paying for everything I have learned in those forty years. My job is to get them fish and so that is what we do. If they think it is they who are the great fisherman it will please them and they will come back next year and ask for us again." He sighed, sat back, sipped his beer and then said "Do not forget, sometimes we have charters like the one today, but other times we have respectful people. Some love our country and come back year after year after year, not just for the fishing, but because they respect our people. I cannot complain."

"Yes, *capitan*, it is because I am younger that I am not as tolerant of them. I do not like the way they think I am inferior to them just because they have a great deal of money. They always think they know more than we do. We are dumb Mexicans and they are smart *Americanos*, and what really bothers me most is they always think we are trying to cheat them somehow. Like the little one today, he was very unhappy when he lost that fish. I thought he was trying to blame you."

"Oh, yes he wanted to blame anyone. But it was not just because we are Mexicans. Loosing the fish might make him look bad. It is not the fishing that worries him; it is the desire to be seen as a bigger man than he is.

Did you see his wife when they were dropped off at the dock this morning?"

"See her, how could I not see her? She walked with him down to the boat and every man on the dock was looking at those legs and breasts. And she knew it, too. She is far younger than him... Is she his big marlin?"

"Something like that."

"Ah captain, you see a lot. Is that why you made that small circle and caused him to lose the fish?"

"No Lorenzo. If I had wanted to I could have done that to please the big one and get a big tip. But I do not do those things. I am paid to get fish for them and that is what I try to do. Do you remember when the big marlin made his first jump and walked across the water on his tail?"

"Of course. It was so far out after the first run that the *Americano* thought it was some other fish jumping until told him it was his, and that he had to bring in all that line to land it. I saw on his face a fear that he did not have the strength, but a determination to do it."

"Yes I too saw that, and it pleased me. He

was determined to get the fish so he could prove how good a fisherman he was. I wanted to see him land that big one. You see, you also saw that determination, Lorenzo. You are learning how to read our customers now. But I also saw something else from my place on the fly bridge, higher over the water. I saw that the fish was not well hooked. As the marlin skipped over the water shaking his head I was afraid he would throw the hook. That is why I made the circle. I wanted to ease the tension a little and give the fisherman a chance to gain some line without letting the fish have a straight pull to break away. Lorenzo, our only job is to help the fisherman catch the fish."

"And the white bearded one with the big blonde wife… that did not matter? It was because the fish was lost that he won the money, and more than that, it made the little one look bad, particularly with his beautiful young wife."

"It is not my job to change the Americans." As I said, some are better than others,

Across the sand, at the table near the water, the grilled *Camarones al mojo de ajo* had been delivered by the waiter and were being washed down with cold local beer by the young couple, to the rhythm of Mariachi music. White breakers, reflecting the lights of the Malecon sparkled in the darkness of the Gulf.

OLD IKE

Brrr, that water is cold! You would think by
June it would have warmed up more than this.
These chest waders are supposed to be
insulated but I can feel the cold coming right
through. As the sun rises above the ridge, and
gets down to me down here in the bottom of
the canyon, the air will warm up anyway,
although it won't help the water temperature.
But that is still a couple of hours away. Never
mind the cold, I'll work my way out a little
deeper and I should be able to drop a fly right
in that big pool on the other side of the river.
Maybe there will be some bigger trout in
there. The two rainbows in my creel are
small, but they will be good eating. But the
big pool on the other side is the place. "Ike's

Pool" Jim calls it.

Jim can't seem to think of anything else except Old Ike. Last night, every time he opened another beer, he had to tell the story again about the time he hooked Ike. "That Old Ike is down there waiting for me." He repeats each time we make the trek to the cabin. "I'm going to hook him again tomorrow, and this time I'm going to land him. It's like he's challenging me. Old Ike against Old Jim, I guess it is."

I've heard it many times, but now I'm getting more worried about Jim. He's slowing down, or course, but that isn't unusual. He's ten years older than I am. He's entitled to take it easier. He's done tough physical work all his life, and even as small and wiry as he is, he's strong. And it's not just the drinking. He's always done that, as long as I can remember. And he is still pretty nimble. Even the broken hip the doctors had to leave a pin in doesn't slow him down much. But he seems to be slowing mentally. I guess that shouldn't be a surprise. It's not just that he is getting older, but he puts away a couple of six packs every day of his life. All that booze can't be doing much for his brain. And every time he gets a few he starts to tell the same stories, as though I hadn't even been there with him when they happened. Twenty years I've gone hunting and fishing with Jim, and now he's telling me about it as though it was a new story each time.

I sure would like to hook Old Ike! Wouldn't that get Jim's attention? I come down here fishing and he's still in the sack. I can see the look on his face. I'd take that fish up to the cabin and lay it in the refrigerator, and not say anything until he went to get milk for his coffee. There would be Old Ike, lying all the way across the second shelf, right below the milk carton. It's been two years since Jim says he hooked Ike. Now that's all he can talk about every time we come up here. It's as though Ike is the biggest trout that anyone ever saw.

I guess with this low light I should put on a bigger fly. Maybe a number twelve Rio Grande King will do it. It's still a little early for a good hatch over the water, but I saw a couple of nice swirls at the far side of the pool, so they are rising for something. Now, strip off some more line, lots of room for a back cast, and lay that line out just as far as you can. Don't get into the brush just upstream, though. Try to put the fly at the top of the pool and get a natural drift down over the deepest part. Ah. Perfect. It dropped right in that little riffle at the top of the pool, and this side of the big rock. The drift should take it just about right, with no drag if I handle it carefully. Make it look natural. Careful, though. Keep out the slack so you don't lose control. Good.

I wonder if Ike is really in there and watching my fly drift overhead. In fact, I wonder if Ike even exists except in Jim's mind. Jim swears he saw him roll at his fly two other times, since the time he says he hooked him, but that he wouldn't take the fly. Jim, says that fish is just "Too damned smart" to be fooled again. It's like an obsession with Jim now. "Ike, Ike, Ike." He swears he is going to catch Old Ike if it's the last thing he ever does. The way Jim has been going lately it may well be. I'm thinking his fishing days are about over.

Whoa! That was some hit. He came right

off the bottom and just gulped in the fly. Now set the hook, but easy, that is a light leader. Don't break him off. I need to keep the rod tip high and let him fight the bend of the rod, not a straight pull at that light tapered leader. He's big! This is one monster trout. I never really saw him, except the roll of his back as he took the fly, but I can tell he's really big. The little trout shiver on the end of the line, with a high-pitched vibration. The bigger trout are a lower frequency; kind of shaking the line as they cut through the water and try to throw the hook. But this one is different. He is just weight and strength. There is no shiver or shake, just solid movement. I can feel the leader singing to me, though. It must be near the breaking point, the way it hums. I'll just ease off on him a little and let him work against the line for a while. Just as long as I can keep him away from that big log at the far end of the pool I should be okay. This is one fish I don't want to lose. I wonder if it could really be Jim's Ike.

All right, fella, take a little line but not too much. Let's see if I can get you coming toward me. Oops, sorry, don't panic. Just don't go too far in that direction. Swing toward me and maybe I can gain some line. Keep away from that log! Don't run any further. Ah, good. Now I can feel you coming toward the surface. Are you going to jump? Go ahead, but don't throw the hook. Ah, here you come…up, up …Oh my God! It's you Ike. Jim wasn't lying. You are magnificent. Don't shake your head that way, or I'm going to lose you. I'm glad I switched to the bigger hook. Why don't you go back down to the deeper water and sulk a bit and I will try to get you closer to me. You are a smart old devil, Ike, but I have to land you. Jim will never believe me if you get away. That's it, now Ike, come a little closer to me on each run; let me get another look at you. I can see you over the gravel. You are beautiful, with those spots on your sides and that tail is so wide it is cutting the surface. It's as wide as an oar blade. No! don't run again! Oh, all right, but not so far next time. Just let me ease you up toward me. Sorry about that hook in your lower jaw, Ike. I bet you have done this many times in your life, and always won. You and Jim. Old timers stalking one another. Do you think about him the way he thinks about you? Do you remember the time you had him on the line but then broke free? You are two tough old guys.

Every run is shorter now, and it won't be long before I will be able to slip my net under you, Ike. There now, I'll keep the rod nearly vertical so all you have to fight is the bend of the rod and I will move you in close. Ike, you are one fine fish. Jim, wasn't lying when he told me about you. I wonder if you remember my friend Jim. He's the guy that hooked you right in this pool a couple of years ago. He's a short wiry guy that walks with a limp. He's up in the cabin now, sleeping There was a time when he would have been down here, but Jim is getting kind of tired. You know, Ike, he said you were too smart to take a fly again. Maybe you are getting tired too. Tell you what, Ike, let's get that little fly out of the corner of your mouth and you can go back to your pool. I won't tell if you don't.

OLD BUDDIES

"Hey Eddie, how about pouring me another beer? Good, put it my tab. Okay? Place looks kind of empty today. Business slowing down?"

"Are you kidding? He couldn't get along without me. Besides the kid he had crewing for him earlier in the season seems to have developed some other interests. Got a girlfriend I guess. So Phil had to come back to the old guy, me. But, yeah, I guess I forgot, we came in earlier than usual today. Had a really interesting fishing charter today."

"Yeah, how come?"

"Let me tell you. This was a different bunch. You think I'm old? We had five guys out for Stripers and Blues and every one of them was pushing eighty, maybe even pushing down from up above. Like usual we were fishing out of Barnstable Marina, so the first thing we did was to head for the back side of Sandy Neck, where they really have been hot for the last week. You work your way down to the East, toward the Sandwich end of the Canal, and there have been lots of Blues and Stripers all the way along, running in schools. Not big, but keepers, and lots of them. Schoolies. Phil is good. He spots the schools, runs over to them and then just kind of works the edges so he doesn't spook them. Great for the customers, with the terns screaming overhead and diving all around the boat, and the fish rolling on the surface, chasing sand eels and hitting blindly at anything that looks like food. The customers, and even Phil and me, get about as worked up as the fish and the birds. If it was just me and Phil it would be great to just drift in and cast for them, but with five old duffers it didn't seem like too hot an idea to have them all flinging big plugs with three needle-sharp treble hooks each around the boat and around our heads. So we just trolled along, picking up lots of fish.

"We've been out maybe three hours. 'Fish on!' hollers the big guy with the beard, Charlie. He might be the youngest, but not by much I would guess, and like the others, knows his fishing. He seems to sit or stand back and watch all the rods and yells every time there's another strike. Sort of like the spotter. Then the next guy up takes the rod. They take turns so the last guy to catch a fish moves back out of the fighting chair and goes back towards the cabin, and the group rotates. So there are usually four in chairs and one leaning up against the back of the cabin. Or at least that is the plan, but by now we have a bunch of fish in the box, and I can see they are all looking kind of tired.

'Okay, Frank, it's your turn ' says the guy they call Rick.

'No, you take it Rick.' He says.

'I just got one, right before Dean got that bigger one.'

'Then how about you, John Mark? You want it?"

'Nope. It's your fish. I wouldn't want to spoil your fun, Frank. Show us how it's done.'

"It isn't often I hear customers trying to get out of taking the rod, but it's not often we get a group like this. Don't get me wrong. They are old, but they are not amateurs at fishing. It seems they have been fishing together, off and on, since they were kids. So by now Frank has taken the rod and is working the fish. Of course, Phil owns the boat and is the captain, so he is up on the flybridge watching and maneuvering, while I am down in the cockpit with these guys, handling baits and rods. So part of my job is to help to land the fish, and if necessary to even help in the catching process, pushing up on the rod or swinging the chair toward the fish. I am supposed to make sure everything is safe, comfortable and enjoyable for them.

"But these guys don't seem to need much technical help. They know what they are doing. They tell me they have been fishing all their lives, and lots of times together, here on Cape Cod, but way back when they were kids. This is like a reunion. But what bothers me is not their ability but their physical condition. Maybe they were once athletes, but now they are more like couch potatoes. So far the fish have been good ones but not huge. But what happens, I'm thinking, if someone hooks into a really big fish? And this one guy, Rick, who seems to be host for the trip, keeps telling me about how he wants to better his lifetime Striper best. It seems he once, when he was much younger, had caught a Striped Bass that went over fifty pounds and won him a big trophy in some tournament. He figures he can still handle a fish like that. Yeah! That I want to see. He's old enough to be my father, and must spend a lot of time in front of the TV. If he caught a trophy Striper it must have been a while back.

"Frank had lifted the rod out of the holder after the line had snapped down from the outrigger. It trembled and wove from side to side in the water, like another Bluefish about the same size. Frank is the biggest of these guys and from what is said I gather he is the oldest. They all look to be a bit past their prime but this one, Frank was the fisherman that, when they showed up at the dock at six in the morning, was the guy that worried me. He was leaning on the shoulder of the smaller man, Dean, and had to be kind of helped down the ramp to the float, it being close to low tide and therefore a steep drop. Getting him into the boat was another chore. His knees seemed hardly able to hold him up. He kind of laughed and apologized, saying he has had surgery on both of them and it didn't seem to have worked too well. Of course, he was a bit overweight which couldn't have helped. But we kind of lifted and guided him into the cockpit and to one of the fishing chairs. He flopped into the chair with a big grin on his face. He was ready to go. But I saw later, believe me he wasn't about to be shown up by the other guys. After we got into fish he was able to get up and move as we went through the rotation. Nevertheless, when it came to his turn to be the guy standing I noticed he was always given a chair. It was just understood he always had a seat. And he always did a good job of landing his fish when his turn came around.

'You okay?' I ask.

'Never better, George.' He says as he starts to crank. But I sure am watching this guy's face. 'He's big and rugged, with a great grin when he isn't hooked up, but when he has a fish on he's all business. It looks like he is in pain, but he sure isn't ready to quit. And, of course, all those old guys are the same. No way they are going to let the others know if they are fading. It's like they don't want to admit they are getting on in years, at least to the others. But I can see they are all pretty well bushed.

So Frank lands it and it's a nice Bluefish, but not as big as the one that the guy they called John Mark had gotten some time earlier. About then Phil calls down to me he wants a bottle of cold water from the cooler, and would I bring it up to him. Usually I would just toss it to him, so I know he wants to talk. So I climb the ladder to the flybridge and stand where the guys can't hear what we are saying, and I kind of let Phil know that these guys have had a good day of fishing already, and I'm a little concerned. He doesn't say anything but kind of nods and goes back to the controls and I go back below. I can see there are lots more fish showing on the surface off to the East, pretty far away. It seemed to have cooled down a lot where we were, but you know how that goes. They pop up somewhere and then they disappear and show up somewhere else, chasing bait and bringing in the terns over them, squawking and diving. We did go down about a mile and picked up; another few fish, but then I noticed that Phil had started to head up West and the fishing went to nothing. That's not like Phil, but I guess he was worried about maybe showing up back at the dock with a couple of cardiac patients instead of happy fishermen.

'There's been some big stripers showing up on the West side of the bay, just north of Billingsgate, in the deep water.' he hollers down over the noise of the revved up engines. 'Bring the lines in and let's go see. Up there off the white cliffs at Wellfleet. We'll finish up; by trolling deep in there and then head for home. We got a bunch of good eating fish in the box already. Let's look for a big one.' Yeah, I thought, and these old duffers can take a breather. Sure there are big fish off Wellfleet, but they are as scarce as hen's teeth.

"So after a high speed run across the bay we put out four lines, two flat lines and two off the outriggers, and go to a slow troll, running the lures real deep. The deepest was a plastic eel on a flat line in the starboard rod holder. By now it's about noon. It's hot in the sun, and there isn't any shade in the cockpit. Besides it's about naptime for those old birds. They had each had a sandwich and a soda on the way across and I can see they are all about to nod off. I'm leaning back against the cabin trying to find a little shade and not too bright-eyed myself when the deep line goes off. Charlie sings out again 'Fish on!' It's not hard to know when you have a good one on. The line goes out fast and steady and with the clicker engaged on the reel it sounds like a high-speed machine gun. This one was like that, times two. 'Holy Shit!' I holler and jump for the rod. But before I can get there Frank has already pulled it out of the holder and is back in his chair. The rod had been right in front of him. It was his turn again, and I noticed he didn't offer the task to someone else this time.

'Let him run. Just keep that rod tip up and make sure he doesn't get any slack' I tell Frank, just like I would any customer. 'Let him fight the rod, not you.'

'I know George." He says, but not like he's mad, just like he doesn't want to be bothered. So I take another look at him to make sure he's all right. All I see is determination. Already he's sweating and he's pulled way back in the chair, straining to hold the rod up.

So after he's straining away for a few minutes I say. 'Frank, do you want me to help you? I could take the rod for a while if you want. Are you okay?'

'You'll get this rod out of my cold dead hands.' He says with a big grin. So, okay, it's his fish. I stand back to watch and Phil is moving the boat so the line is straight astern. By now the other flat line is brought in by Charlie and I go back to get the outrigger lines out of the way. I know, and I guess so does Phil, that this is no ordinary school striper, and we sure don't want to lose it. So I keep looking at Frank and wondering if he can hold out.

"And then, so help me God, you wouldn't believe what that old guy does. He stands up! He gets up on those wobbly legs and moves to the transom. 'I have never fished from a chair before.' He says. 'I'm used to standing up when I fish.' I was thinking he was going to go over the stern, rod and all, because he sure as hell wasn't about to let go of that rod. But then came the real surprise. If you could call an overweight old guy who needs a shave, is covered in sweat, is shaking with the strain of holding that rod, beautiful, he was beautiful, at least in the eyes of a fellow fisherman. I felt like I was in the presence of a master! Amateurs let the fish control them. They bend forward toward the fish, awkward and off balance, and do much more work than they should. Real masters let the fish fight the rod and the weight of the fisherman. Amateurs use too much energy and they use it at the wrong time. Pros only work when it is productive. They sense when they can gain line and when they can't.

"Just watching this guy I could tell he had been fishing lots of years, and knew his business. He shifted his weight back and bent those troublesome knees so that he balanced his body weight against the pull of the fish. He became the center support of a seesaw. He shifted back and forth in response to the increased or decreased pull on the line. He let the fish wear itself out and then he cranked it in, but only cranked when he knew he could gain line. Hell, I'm half the age of the guy but let me tell you, Eddie, I couldn't have done it half as well. So I got out of the way and let him perform. No way was I going to touch anything until I could grab the wire leader. It was his fish, landed or lost. But the way he handled it I could see he wasn't going to lose it, at least not without a fight. And finally he had the fish alongside, so I grabbed the leader with one hand and the gaff in the other and hauled that baby into the boat. But it wasn't easy. It was a huge Striper, hammering his tail, as wide as an oar blade, against the floorboards.

'That's it, we're heading in.' bellows Phil from up above. 'Time's about up anyway and I want to get that fish to an official scale as quick as we can. Keep dousing it with water so it won't dry out and lose weight.' I look over first to Frank. He's slumped in the chair with his eyes closed but with the biggest grin you ever seen. Then I look over at the others, his buddies that didn't get a big one, and they have grins that are just as big.

"Well, we get back to the marina ASAP and take the fish up to the scales in the office, and he weighs in at fifty-five pounds, even. And the guy, Rick, who had been bragging earlier about his tournament winning fish says 'Damn, Frank, you beat my big one by a measly two pounds.' But you could see he couldn't have been happier. Same for the other guys.

"Draw me another beer, Eddie."

THE LAST MARLIN

I usually don't have much contact with the short timers. That is because they come and go, constantly changing, but I'm here for the entire season. We come down to Mexico in the early Fall and stay until late Spring, but most of them are just here for a week or two. Renters, while we own our place. That is why I am kind of surprised I even got to know this guy. Maybe he got my attention that first day, because I was there when they showed up. I happened to be down in the lobby area of the Condo, just having come in from a walk along the beach that the condo fronts on, so I was wearing shorts, a grey tee shirt and flip-flops, and of course my baseball cap. My bald head and my light complexion burn easily in this tropic sun. But that doesn't keep me off the water every chance I get. I have a boat down at the marina, so I spend a great deal of my time there, talking pigeon Spanish but mostly English with the Mexican fishing people. Just about any afternoon you can find me sipping a beer with them at the cantina by the boat docks. Usually some of us have been out fishing since early morning and have just come in, sometimes with smaller fish, but often with a Mahi-Mahi, what the Mexicans call a Dorado, and occasionally, if someone has been really lucky, a Yellowfin Tuna or a Striped Marlin. My wife says I would rather be with my buddies at the marina than with the other Americans and Canadians at the Condo, and maybe she is right.

So it was somewhat unusual that I was not at the marina that Thursday afternoon. Usually I preferred to get home later in the afternoon, then walk the beach, and finally watch the sunset while soaking in the community hot tub with, as with the other regulars, a drink in a plastic cup. Later the two of us occasionally would go to a close by

Mexican restaurant for some supper. But this day I had come back earlier than usual.

It really was his lady that got my attention first. Small, slim, dark complexion, and lovely. I thought she must be quite bit younger than the man with her. She obviously had been here before, although I did not remember her. But she was chatting gaily in Spanish with the young girl behind the desk, and looking at pictures of the attendant's new baby. I looked closer. She was not that young, but she obviously paid close attention to her appearance, both in her clothing and her make-up. She made me think of a model in the way she walked in. My first thought was to wonder what she was doing with him. Perhaps he was rich. They were obviously not married. I could automatically reach that conclusion by just having seen them get out of the cab. He held the door for her and held her hand an instant as he guided her out of the rear seat. They smiled at one another while the driver pulled out their suitcases. In the lobby, before she had greeted the girl at the desk they had briefly held hands. No, I knew they were not married. And she was a looker! What could she see in him?

I turned my attention to the man. He was a large man, but neither skinny nor overweight. He gave the impression of a man who had been fit and athletic but had aged beyond it.   I thought of a front yard snowman that had stood too long in the sun on a warm day. My guess was that he was in his mid-seventies, which I was to find out later, was well away from his actual octogenarian status. As I studied him I wished I had had his head of hair! Even though it was white; he had lots of it; it was parted and neat. His face was clean-shaven and lined with deep creases. Dark eyes and a straight nose over a pleasant smile. He appeared contented. But he looked pale in comparison to most of the people I was seeing daily, as though he did not get enough sun.   You could tell they were just arriving because he was in travel clothes. That is, he had long dress trousers rather than shorts or jeans, and a neatly pressed sports shirt. His shoes belied either his affectation or affection for the water, since they were rubber soled boat shoes. And he rocked now from one of those shoes to the other, obviously somewhat an impatient man, I thought. After waiting a while as she continued to chat, he left the suitcases in the middle of the lobby and retreated to the heavy overstuffed leather chairs, where he first leaned against one of them, obviously resting, and finally sat heavily in it. He seemed very tired even though he had done no more than roll in a suitcase. As I started back to our place I saw that she had finished their conversation, and presumably they were going to their rental.

It was two nights later that I encountered them again. It was sunset; we and the other regulars were soaking in the hot tub, when they approached in bathing suits, carrying towels and with plastic cups filled with what appeared to be red wine. Again, I noticed her first, wearing a small and colorful bikini which showed vividly the slim figure I had guessed at before. And he was wearing a boxer bathing suit that looked too large and too colorful. His legs were heavy, not spindly as one might expect in an older man, but untanned and somewhat flabby, giving again the impression of a fading physique. Immediately my gregarious wife greeted then and motioned them to join us.

He happened to lower himself into the steaming water right beside me, so we began to talk. Strangely, I found myself liking the guy. For one thing he was a fisherman. So we talked fishing. We compared experiences, both fresh and salt water, in both my native Canada as well as his America, and even in other parts of the world. Everything from King Salmon to Rainbow Trout, from Largemouth Bass to Grayling to Tuna. Between us we had done a lot of fishing in a lot of places. In the meantime his lady was a big hit with the others. They chatted and laughed and sipped their wine. She seemed too genuine and candid to be the gold digger I had first imagined, and maybe this guy did have some appeal. I mean, a fisherman might have other good features, I thought.

Of course the conversation turned to local fishing. It turned out he was hoping to charter a boat and go out just once during his brief stay. I told him that we were getting some nice Mahi-Mahi, but that the Marlin had not showed up much yet. Perhaps the water was not warm enough for them. But they were due. He seemed somewhat disappointed in that, but then shrugged and said he would love going for Mahi-Mahi, and, laughing, that it was perhaps all that he could handle at his age, anyway. Well, I know most of the charter captains, and see them come in each day, with or without fish, and I often share a beer with some of them in the Cantina, so I know who is good and who isn't. So I offered to introduce him to David. David and his boat boy, Felipe, are the best, I think. Born and brought up right here they have both spent much of their lives on the water, and they both speak good English, although I found out later that it was not an issue; both he and his lady speak excellent Spanish. But David has the instinct. He can find the fish when few others do. He knows those waters intimately, and locates where he wants to put his lures when it just seems like any other patch in that big Gulf. I assured him that David was the one, and arranged to meet him at the marina the next day. She would be going fishing with him, I learned.

So that is how it was that we were sitting at
the Cantina the next afternoon, enjoying a
cold one and some salsa and chips. She had
come along with him, and I had seen
repeatedly that she would instinctively reach
for him if there was break in the crumbling
sidewalk where she thought he might trip.
Yet he was not at all feeble, but perhaps a
little unsteady. The sun was reflecting off the
water, and off the masts of the sailboats at our
left. To the right the charter boats were lined
up, stern to the docks, many being washed
down and emptied of fish boxes and other
gear. We had been down to the big black-
hulled one nearest to the ramp and talked to
David. As usual cheerful, he worked as we
talked. I introduced my friends and asked
him if he was free for the next day. It turned
out he was. I let the two of them do the
arrangements, but I had already made it clear
to David that these people, although *Turistas*
should get a good deal. It was set for seven
the next morning. So we had come back up
to the coolness of the metal tables under the
thatched roof of the Cantina. He of course
thanked me, and then surprised me by saying,

"Why don't you come along? The boat can accommodate more than just two fishermen, it's paid for anyway, and we would enjoy your company." So, why not, I accepted. It was agreed we would meet in the lobby the next morning and go back down to the marina in my car.

To me the best part of a day of fishing is the early morning start. I love the sounds of the marina, in the darkness, as other crews prepare to go, their voices drifting across the water. Often there is hot coffee in a thermos. So I delighted in the slow motoring out of the confines of the harbor in the darkness, and then the sun just starting to push away the dark and coloring the water and silhouetting the shoreline behind us, with just scattered lights of early risers. David was a shadow, his face aglow from the instrument panel, standing at the controls on the fly bridge and Felipe was already rigging baits, untangling lines, readying the outriggers and setting rods in the holders. Looking over I saw the same pleasure in the two of their faces also. She was taking pictures but he was just silently taking it all in, as though memorizing the scene.

Two hours later we were out of sight of land, and trolling back and forth along an imaginary line on the water that was evidently visible only to David. We had been persisting fruitlessly for some time, but David and Felipe did not seem to get discouraged. The lady was below and my friend was up on the flybridge talking to David while I was relaxed in one of the two fighting chairs when the first strike came, snapping the line off the Starboard outrigger. So, being the nearest, it was my fish. Before long I worked in a beautiful Dorado, perhaps twenty-five pounds. Supper!

After a few more passes David moved the boat further out, looking for exactly the watercolor he wanted. It wasn't long before the next blind strike occurred. But this one was different. It seemed to come up from directly below, and we saw the unmistakable bill of a marlin thrashing the water as he took the bait. We quickly got the lady into the chair and she settled down to work, and it was impressive that such a small and petite a person could show so much strength.

Understand, these are not big swivel chairs bolted to the deck and fitted with heavy harnesses or straps to clip to the reel. The chair just has a gimbaled socket for the butt of the rod. So that means holding the rod entirely with the strength of one arm while reeling with the other. And that was what she was doing. But we both had to talk to her about pumping the fish in, pulling back to gain line and then the leaning forward and reeling to retrieve the gain. Her long red painted nails on the upper rod and the reel handle and her small sneakered feet braced against the fish box seemed out of place, but there was no doubt, looking at her set features under the brim of her white baseball cap, that she was intent on the job. Once instructed she worked the fish well and we soon boated a fine seven foot long Striped Marlin. She was proud and pleased at what she told us was her first marlin, and I could see also the pride and happiness on his face. Soon the captain came down from the bridge and shook her hand.

It was late in the day before he got his turn. I had been afraid he was going to miss out, and David was instructing Felipe to start to put away some of the gear. We were the furthest out from shore we had been and it would be a long trip back in. David, in his high perch saw it first and motioned to Felipe. The long dark shadow of a marlin, cruising on the surface was soon   visible to starboard. Heading in the opposite direction to us were a pair of black spikes protruding from the water, the dorsal fin and the tail of a large fish. Just a glance told me they were unusually far apart, indicating size.   David was not hasty but decisive in turning into a course that would parallel and then intercept the direction the   marlin   was   headed.   They   were businesslike, but I sensed the excitement. They knew this was a good one if we could hook it. By then my friend was in the fighting chair. There was no hesitation or indecision. The big marlin saw the bait on the portside flat line, turned, accelerated and slammed it. Felipe   had   second-guessed   him   and immediately had the rod out of its holder, leaned back twice to set the hook, pushed the notched stainless steel butt of the rod into the socket on the seat of the fighting chair and transferred control of the fight. Our first marlin had run a short distance, jumped three times, tail walking majestically, and then staged his battle near the boat. This one headed for the horizon, stripping line off the reel and putting tremendous pressure on his tormentor. My friend could do no more than hold on and strain to keep the rod up as the line disappeared. I looked down at him. His face was red and his eyes were squinting in the effort to hold the fish. He tried to slow or stop the run, to no avail, and finally stopped trying to reel, but did not loosen the drag. Eventually the fish stopped his run, rose to the surface and jumped just once to show us what we were up against It was all that was needed for us to see how big he was and how far away he was. At this point I glanced upward and saw that David was gesturing to Felipe from above and pointing to the fisherman. Felipe quickly looked closely at the man, like a ref looking at a fighter who has taken too many punches, and then indicated that he should take the rod and give him some help. "Dejelo! It's my fish." he almost yelled, and waved Felipe away. Felipe shrugged and looked back up to David, who returned the shrug, smiled and returned to keeping the boat in position.

I looked again, wondering if my friend was in any condition to handle it. The muscles that were straining so now had seemed to me earlier to have been hanging and flabby on his arms and his hands were, one could easily see, twisted with arthritis. In his face I saw first a look of despair as he realized how much line he would have to retrieve, and as I watched the expression seemed to change to one of determination, and then to a half smile. I realized that he was enjoying himself immensely even as he was straining painfully. Then I realized she was right beside him, her hand on his shoulder and watching him closely. I saw worry but I also saw something else, call it love I guess. She evidently knew this man and respected his tenacity, even if it might be foolish. Again I adjusted my thoughts about her.

We entered the hard work phase. He did it well, but I could see it was painful. First he was raising the rod with one hand and reeling on the down move with the other As he tired he switched to a two hand raise and then reel as he dropped the tip. He was careful, though, to guide the line with his thumb so that it would lie evenly on the reel not bunch up. Occasionally he would stop entirely and let the fish just fight the tight line while he dangled his left hand beside him, perhaps to restore the circulation or perhaps to relieve cramping. But he did get it done, and would not allow anyone to help until Felipe could reach over the stern, grab the leader, and finally grasp the bill of the thrashing fish and slide him, still twisting and lunging, into the boat. It wasn't the biggest Striped Marlin I have ever seen taken but it was right up there. He slumped back in the chair, closed his eyes for a few seconds but then insisted on having pictures taken. He had told David he preferred "catch and release" but the fish was too badly injured. Then David came down, congratulated him on the fine fight and we headed for home.

It was some time later that I left the bridge, where I had been talking to David, and went back down the ladder to the cockpit. Felipe was cleaning and fileting my Mahi-Mahi and getting the boat organized as we neared land. The two of them had retreated to the shade and comfort to the cabin. I looked in and saw that he was lying on the sofa at the right, and she was sitting beside him with his head in her lap. I hesitated to intrude but she motioned me in. His eyes were closed, and now the earlier redness of his face had turned to an ashen paleness that startled me. But he opened his eyes, smiled and told me to join them.

"Perfect," He said. "A perfect day on the water. I can't thank you enough for setting it up for us."

"He shouldn't have been doing this you know." She said, but not in anger or rebuke, perhaps in resignation. She was smiling and looked down at him. " He's a walking time bomb, with all those stents in his heart. But we make our choices."

"It's really strange, though. Last night I woke up long before daybreak, and got to thinking about going fishing today, just like I used to as a kid. And somehow I knew I was going to hook a marlin today. Oh yes, you had told me they were not in, but strangely I knew. I started to believe there was one out here waiting for me. And then I got to wondering if I was still up to it. I wanted one more marlin in my life. Before I got back to sleep I had determined I was going to do it if it killed me."

"And I was afraid it was going to," She said softly as though I were not there.

"Yes, we do make our choices." He said. "That's my last marlin, you know."

ABOUT THE AUTHOR

Richard W. (Dick) Arms has spent a long career studying, writing about, and analyzing Stock Markets from the standpoint of a Technical Analyst. His Arms Index , his charting methods of Equivolume and Arms Candlevolume and his the many innovations in analysis, presented in his many books, have changed the way in which investors look at the interplay of price and volume in the markets. From his home in Albuquerque he still writes timely stock market columns and an Advisory letter for Institutional Money Managers.

However, Dick has also, over the years, written works of fiction and has also spent many wonderful days fishing, with many interesting people. These characters have helped him to combine these two interests into this collection of short stories.

Also by Richard W. Arms

Non-fiction

Profits in Volume
The Arms Index
Volume Cycles in the Stock Market
Trading without Fear
Stop and Make Money

Fiction

Kokopelli

Want more?

Be sure to visit Belfort & Bastion's webpage
at:

BelfortandBastion.com

for more cutting edge fiction, non-fiction,
poetry, and prose.

Made in the USA
San Bernardino, CA
26 April 2016